HOSTAGE BRIDE

"You can't get away with it; my father will surely find out about everything."

"Perhaps...but not immediately...and that's what is vital to success. We'll be on that ship tomorrow, Charlotte—as man and wife."

"How do you know? I just might call your bluff."

His lazy, catlike glance once more lingered on my face, stroking it with the deliberateness of a languid caress. He said softly, "I know you very well, Charlotte," and reached out and took my hand.

His intimate tone brought color rushing hotly up into my cheeks. He held my eyes and managed to make me feel naked before his bold gaze. It was impossible! I hated this stranger...and yet his touch was sending warmth spiraling through my flesh. "You're the devil," I gasped, jerking my hand away.

Other *Leisure Books* by Leona Karr:
OBSESSION

Illusions

LEONA KARR

LEISURE BOOKS NEW YORK CITY

A LEISURE BOOK®

February 1994

Published by

Dorchester Publishing Co., Inc.
276 Fifth Avenue
New York, NY 10001

Printed in the United States of America.

To Kate Moulder,
whose encouragement led me to write romantic fiction.

Illusions

1

My luggage had been sent ahead and had already been loaded on the Lucania for her scheduled departure the next afternoon from New York's busy Pier J. The trim ocean vessel was a new addition to the Cunard Line and possessed all the latest comforts in sea travel this spring of 1893. It was arranged that my Cousin Della would meet my late afternoon train from Philadelphia and we would spend the night in her brownstone home and then board the new ocean liner for a delightful crossing and month's tour of the British Isles.

I took a deep breath as the train from New Jersey eased into the New York station. In a nervous gesture, I smoothed the brown folds of my serge traveling dress with its wide collar and velvet piping and vigorously tucked some wayward russet wisps of hair under my bonnet.

I wore a fawn-colored carriage cloak for the day was gray and chilly; the skies were overcast with intermittent rain peppering against the dirty train windows.

The inclement weather had not dampened my spirits. I knew my face was flushed with excitement and there was a quiver of nervousness in the pit of my stomach. I had traveled the short journey from Philadelphia to New York many times on the New York Central Railroad—but never alone. The elderly porter had looked surprised when I boarded without a companion. Even now I felt numerous eyes on me questioning the propriety of an unattended young woman of nineteen sitting alone in a plush seat of an ornate parlor car. The train's decor was more gaudy than genteel as competing railroads tried to lure passengers from one line to another with their ostentatious decorations and rather uncomfortable upholstered seats. I was grateful that my journey was a short one.

My father had intended to accompany me to New York. I remembered how upset he was when asked to replace a university colleague who had suddenly been taken ill during a conference. My father was a Professor of Letters, educated in England where he had met and married my mother. They had returned to the United States after graduation. Most of his academic life had been spent at Pennsylvania University and I had been born and raised in the shadows of those ivory towers. My mother had died when I was three years old in an influenza epidemic that nearly took my life also. My father and I were extremely close and this would be the first time I had been away from him for any extended period of time. Although Cousin Della had been promising to take me with her on some of her travels, this was the first time she had ever issued a specific invitation. I was excited and scared at the same time. It would have been reassuring to have my father see us off on the ocean liner.

Well, it couldn't be helped. I knew my father couldn't have refused the Dean's request to take charge of an important seminar at the last minute even though my departure had been set for this date months ago. I had assured him that I could manage to travel that short distance without mishap. After all, he had raised me to be perfectly capable of making decisions and carrying them out. Although disappointed not to have his company to New York and his affectionate "bon voyage" at the dock, I decided not to let him know how nervous I was. I had given his burly, old frame a hug and kissed him goodbye, laughingly assuring him everything was under control.

My Cousin Della was a favorite relative and I had always been in awe of her. While other women were carefully corseted and dared only to add a pastel fichu to a modest gown, her rather plump figure might be draped in some colorful Oriental kimono or an Indian sari. My father had some doubts about her being a proper chaperone for me but I couldn't think of anyone more exciting to have as a travel companion. She was only ten years older than me and a vivacious widow, having traveled all over the globe with her husband before his death two years ago. I was delighted that she had asked me to accompany her to England this spring.

When we reached the New York station and the train groaned to a stop, I disembarked eagerly, looking about for Cousin Della's dark curly head and plump figure. Although the rain had stopped for the moment in some kind of capricious hiatus, puddles of water had already collected along the platform. A late afternoon sun had given up trying to pierce the shroud of rain clouds, and a wash of diffused light was bringing an early twilight to the big city. I gathered the collar of my cloak and hood closer around me.

The train had disgorged its passengers into this gloomy atmosphere and the inhospitable weather had hurried them inside into the congested station. Almost immediately I found myself left nearly alone on the train platform with Cousin Della still nowhere in sight.

"Need some help, Miss?" asked the gray-haired conductor as I lingered near the steps of the train.

I summoned a false smile. "No, thank you. My cousin seems to have been detained . . . I'm sure she'll be here in a moment." I shifted the small portmanteau I held in my hands, debating whether or not I should go into the station to wait. I hesitated. There had been talk of building a new grand terminal to handle the congestion of competing train lines in and out of New York, but at the moment such plans were only on the drawing boards. Without a prearranged meeting place, the chances of finding anyone in the overcrowded station seemed infinitesimal. No, I would wait here on the platform so we wouldn't miss each other.

I paced the length of the parlor car, back and forth in the crisp air, telling myself that any moment a plump, full-faced, middle-aged woman bobbing full steam toward me with apologies flowing from her lips would greet my eyes.

Looking back, I believe the first presentiment of the terror waiting to engulf me slithered to the surface of my mind in those few moments but I readily dismissed it as nervousness over Cousin Della's tardiness. And yet, in some deep recess of my mind, I somehow sensed her delay was ominous. Brushing aside the premonition as absurd, I tried to dismiss the feeling as pure feminine insecurity. Firmly I took myself in hand and tried to decide what I should do under the unexpected circumstances. I had taken hired hacks to Cousin Della's house many times, with my mother as a child and with my father after her death. I shook myself mentally. Of course, that was the sensible thing to do. Instead of drawing attention to myself waiting alone on a station platform, I would hire a hack and give the driver her address. If we missed each other, we would soon be reunited at her fashionable home.

Even as I hesitated, and huddled deep in my cloak, a chill that had nothing to do with the sharp wind rippled up the back of my neck. I could not have told you why but I knew that someone was watching my movements, step by step. I swung my greenish hazel eyes in a wide arc, and even cast some surreptitious glances over my shoulder as I entered the station and pushed my way through the crowd. I scolded myself for such foolishness but a sense of panic remained. I moved at a hurried pace until I finally reached the front entrance and emerged on the sidewalk in front of the station.

The street was congested with vehicles: wagons, drays, pretentious carriages, smart phaetons and small, agile buggies, their painted sides gleaming wet in the light mist and their wheels sending up sprays of water like whirling fountains as they splashed through puddles. The smells of the city were there, sharp and odoriferous, and the drizzle was heavy with smoke. Fancy, high-stepping horses and laboring dray teams clattered down the glistening streets as they shook their harnesses, tossed their heads, and whinnied their displeasure at the cold and rain. Everywhere, disgruntled men ducked down into their coat collars, stuffed their hands into wide pockets and barreled down the wet sidewalks in hunched positions, looking neither right nor left as the city swallowed them up. Coming out of the crowded station or alighting from arriving carriages, fashionable women found themselves inadequately dressed for the inclement weather because they had unwisely chosen style over warmth and their fashionable pelisse coats offered little protection against the blasts of cold air which lifted their skirts and petticoats. They held on to plumed hats which, although anchored with long hat pins, threatened to lift off their heads in the quickening breeze.

A cacophony of sounds greeted my ears. Beggars huddled close to the building, holding out scrawny arms and croaking a "Bless you" when some kind soul dropped a penny or two into their hands. Urchin newspaper boys yelled the headlines of their twopenny newspapers with frosty clouds in front of their blue-tinged lips as they shivered in thin, patched clothes and worn-out shoes. Only a few customers paused in the rain to dig into their pockets to buy the afternoon paper proclaiming President Cleveland's concern over the Franco-Russian Alliance.

Usually I delighted in city sounds and sights. The city noise, riotous color, assaulting smells, and sensual bombardment were exciting; but I had never been alone before in the congestion of indifferent humanity, vulnerable to the insidious evils that were as much a part of New York as the rats which infested the sewers. Brownstone buildings now lost any aura of delight and in the darkening mist seemed to lean forward in a sinister way, as if to trap me. It was still daylight but a valiant sun fought a losing battle in the overwhelming gloom. Gas street lamps and lights in nearby store windows were only pale yellow smudges and held no promise of their usual tempting treasures.

I pushed my way to the curb in front of the station. A wind—raw and malicious—billowed my cloak and made me bend my head against it. I wanted to run and flee—but from what I could not define. I despaired of readily getting a hack but suddenly there was a driver in front of me asking me if I wanted one.

I gave my cousin's address to the emaciated-looking man whose deeply sunken eyes examined me from my bonnet to the tips of my high-buttoned shoes. Any other time I might have hesitated to engage him for anything but I only wanted to get to my cousin's house as quickly as possible.

I bolted into the vehicle with its high wheels and black upholstered seat. When the man shut the door, I sank back with an explosive relief and realized then that my breath was coming in short gasps. With a rising sense of paranoia, I peered out the window, searching once more for anyone who could be sending that disturbing prickling of gooseflesh up my back. Why did the sensation persist? Even as my intense gaze searched the surge of people coming and going through the arched doors, I could not rid myself of the feeling that a stranger was watching me.

With the crack of a whip, we lurched away from the curb. I sank back with such relief that I actually felt giddy. The driver maneuvered through the congested streets and set the horse at a rhythmic trot in the direction of my aunt's brownstone home.

I almost laughed then. Some woman of the world I was! One little complication and my veneer of confidence disappeared. It was obvious that for some mundane reason Cousin Della had been unable to meet the train. Well-laid plans went awry every day and here I was in some kind of panic. I was sure my cousin would meet me at the door of her brownstone and with her usual flutter of hands and flood of chatter explain what had happened. We would laugh about it and I would feel more foolish than ever.

Some of my tension evaporated. Although the first burst of excitement had been tainted by my cousin's failure to meet me, I could understand how it had happened. My Cousin Della lived independently in a home that had been pur-chased years ago when her husband was an officer in the army. They traveled all over the world and brought back treasures until their New York home resembled a museum. After his death, Cousin Della continued to travel but she lived alone in her New York home when resting between journeys. She was the perfect companion for my first trip abroad—or so I thought. Now, a vague suspicion surfaced that dependability might not be one of her traits and I met that revelation with a surge of irritation. Unfortunately, patience was not one of my strong points. I folded my gloved hands in my lap and schooled myself not to let my cousin know how much this little unexpected complication annoyed me. It would not do to start out on a long journey with friction between us.

It was not the scene outside the window that finally alerted me to the fact that I was not being taken directly to my aunt's house because the glass was beaded with moisture and looking through it was like peering through a thick haze. It was the passing of time—the ride from the station to Cousin Della's home was less than twenty minutes. I looked at the lapel watch pinned to my bodice and saw that the train had arrived nearly an hour ago. Even accounting for the wait on the platform, we should have reached Cousin Della's house by now.

My mouth was suddenly dry and my heartbeat lurched into my throat, beating erratically. I tried to get the driver's attention but he ignored me. *Where was he taking me?* I began to suspect then that his arrival at my side had not been by chance. Why should he seek me out when others were clamoring for a hired hack? His thin face with its pointed chin and deep-set dark eyes came back to me and I remembered the way he had scrutinized me. Yes, now I was certain he had pushed through the crowd at the curb to reach me. At the time my relief at getting a hansom cab had dulled any suspicion that he might have been waiting for me. Although I had never been one to succumb to hysterics, I smothered some screams lumped together under my rib cage. Enough tales of white slavery had reached my ears to fuel my rising panic. I knew hundreds of girls disappeared each year in New York City and were never heard from again.

I had to get away . . . but how? The fast-moving vehicle would not allow for any safe exit. Where were we? Should I open the narrow door and scream for help? I feared the wind would drive my cries right back down my throat or whip them away in its high-pitched moaning. I didn't want to alert the driver to my suspicions. No, I had to wait until the hack stopped . . . and then be ready to lunge out the door before the driver could descend from his high perch. I clung to this plan as I clutched my portmanteau and perched on the edge of the seat. Sweat beaded on my forehead and my gloved hands were ice-cold.

It seemed like an eternity but in just a few more moments the vehicle jolted to an abrupt halt. I expedited my plan and flung myself out of the hack, nearly falling on my face, only to find myself in front of my cousin's familiar brownstone house.

Stunned for a moment, I then realized what had happened. The driver had taken a circuitous route in order to collect a bigger fare. My relief was followed immediately by indignation as anxiety dissolved into anger. He had tried his big city tricks on the wrong person! Haughtily I gave him the usual fare, including the tip my father always gave. "I believe that is the correct amount," I said with a toss of my chin.

I expected some haggling and was disappointed when he tipped his cap perfunctorily and replied, "Yes, ma'am." Without giving me another glance, he mounted his high seat and gave a curt "giddy-up" to the horse. The sound of horse hooves faded away down the residential street.

I turned and quickly mounted the steps to Cousin Della's familiar white door with its brass hardware polished and gleaming. I expected the door to open and even had a smile tugging at the corner of my lips as I reached the top step. It faded when the door did not open and there was no sign of welcome.

No hint of movement came from inside the house, no welcoming cry reached my ears, and no warm, embracing arms stretched out to engulf me. The front curtained windows were like dark, glazed eyes. There was only silence. As I stood there in the drizzle, the same sense of foreboding I had felt earlier at the train station came back. Something was wrong. I knew it. A deep uneasiness coated the inside of my mouth with sudden dryness. I was reacting to some indefinable awareness that reached out from the house to warn me.

If only I had turned away then, but I didn't. I

swallowed against the dryness in my mouth and throat and dropped the lion's head knocker with a demanding clang. The familiar sound was reassuring. Hundreds of times I had stood here on the doorstep with my father. The knocker was a cue which brought back memories of happy reunions with my cousin. I willed the door panel to swing open and the imagined scene between myself and Cousin Della would be enacted amid hugs and laughter.

I waited. My hands clutched the bone handle of my small portmanteau so tightly that my knuckles turned white. I braced myself against the misty drizzle and freshening wind, a cold inner chill joining that coming from the inclement weather. Only a waiting silence answered the knocker's brassy clang.

I searched for a rational explanation. Surely, I had somehow missed her at the station and she hadn't returned yet. Yes, that must be it—somehow our paths had crossed and she would turn around and come home and find me here. I shoved away mounting apprehension. Fortunately I had been given a key to the house during one of our former visits when she knew that she was going to be away when my father and I arrived. Thanking God that I didn't have to linger on the doorstep until Cousin Della's return, I dug in my beaded reticule and brought out the skeleton key.

It was only when I had it in my gloved hand that I discovered a startling fact—the door wasn't locked. It swung open easily under my touch. Then my cousin must be home, I thought, relieved. Her house was filled with lovely and expensive imports and artifacts and I knew that Cousin Della would never go anywhere without locking her door.

Eagerly, I stepped into the front hall. "Cousin Della!" I called. Only dim late afternoon light spilled through the open door. My voice echoed in the long hall running from the front vestibule to the back of the house. A wide staircase smelling of a recent polishing of turpentine and beeswax stood against one wall. The carpeted steps were shadowy and unlit as if the waning daylight had taken the house unawares. A lovely chandelier hung darkly from the high ceiling and the colors of an expensive Oriental carpet were lost in the grayness of the foyer.

I slowly closed the door behind me. Long shadows of late afternoon lay possessively on the oak floor and a heavy stillness assaulted my senses.

"Cousin Della . . . It's Charlotte . . . I'm here." My voice floated up the staircase and reverberated with a kind of mocking echo.

An almost palatable silence settled through the house as the sound of my voice faded away. I fought an urge to turn and run. Run where? The sensible question that rose somewhere out of my befuddled mind kept me standing there. Then I saw that one of Della's suitcases and a hat box had been placed at the foot of the staircase. The sight was reassuring and put some sanity back into the situation. She was ready for our trip. She had brought those things down from upstairs. But where was she?

"Cousin Della?" I called again as I dropped my portmanteau beside her suitcase and hatbox.

On the left, my cousin's formal parlor yawned in gray darkness and her lovely Louis XVI and Queen Anne furniture were only indistinct blobs as I peered in and verified what I already knew. The room was unoccupied. A lingering sweetness of Della's jasmine perfume touched my nostrils with a familiar reassurance. I clung to this sensory cue that she had been in the room recently and with my skirts rustling in the echoing stillness, I went expectantly down the hall until I reached another doorway. It opened into Cousin Della's muted green and yellow sitting room which I had always thought to be the most comfortable room in the house.

As I swept in, I willed to see my cousin's plump figure overflowing in her favorite chair with her face beaming her usual warm welcome. I had spent hours in that room with her, looking at souvenirs of her travels and carefully handling pieces of jade or fragile lace and listening to her laughing voice as she related some amusing incident.

An empty room mocked those warm memories. Rain beat against a glass door leading out onto a terrace and the enveloping darkness brought the cold and gloom inside. With trembling hands I turned on a gaslight which spilled a circle of light across the floor.

Nothing seemed amiss. Priceless antiques remained undisturbed in their glass cabinets. Only a seventeenth century mantel clock broke the thick silence with a rhythmic ticking that vibrated loudly in my ears. I resisted a wild urge to scream and break the oppressive silence. For a long moment I stood there frozen.

Then a tiny click like that of dishware being handled brought my head up and I strained to hear an almost imperceptible sound coming from the back of the house. My heart leaped into my throat. The kitchen! Cousin Della was in the kitchen preparing afternoon tea. For some reason she had not heard me come in.

Relief like choking hysteria rose in my throat. I turned and sped down the hall toward the spacious blue and white kitchen where Cousin Della tried out her international recipes. There was light spilling into the hall and a greeting was already forming on my lips as I went through the kitchen doorway—but the words were never spoken. They stuck like hard, jagged pellets in my throat.

A stranger stood at the counter, his back to me. He turned around as I entered. He held two china cups and saucers in his hands and he set them down on the lacy cloth of Della's breakfast table. He seemed to be a man in his thirties, slender but not slight, with jet black hair springing darkly from a broad forehead. His bone structure was crisp and bold and a lightly tanned complexion seemed at odds with his dark frock coat and black trousers.

"I thought you might like a cup of tea after your journey, Charlotte." The words were ordinary but there was nothing soft or gentle in the solicitous remark. The use of my first name was not one of familiarity or friendliness but of ominous intent. His voice was as hard as the gray eyes that bit into mine like tempered steel. My mouth must have worked to try and form some words because he answered my unvoiced question. "There has been a change in plans. Your Cousin Della won't be able to go with you tomorrow, Charlotte . . . so I'll be accompanying you instead."

2

The wind wailed under the eaves of the house, a counterpoint to the sudden terror tightening my chest. I blinked as if he were an apparition that would disappear when sanity returned. Perhaps I was hallucinating; this couldn't be happening. A grim-looking stranger stood in my cousin's kitchen, calling me by my given name. Where was Cousin Della? What did he mean she wouldn't be traveling with me?

"Sit down, Charlotte." This time it was an order, not a polite request. He pulled out a chair for me indicating that he wanted me to sit there.

I did not move. "Who are you?" I croaked. "Where is my cousin?"

"Sit down," he ordered without answering.

"No, not until you tell me what is going on!" I didn't take to bullying even though unadulterated fear had sent a wash of paralyzing weakness through my body.

Black eyebrows over wintry eyes drew together impatiently. "I will . . . as soon as you sit down, Charlotte, and have some tea." There was a hint of violence in his tone and I imagined that it flared readily when anyone dared to question his command. Under other circumstances I might have stubbornly remained standing until I fell from exhaustion but at the moment too many emotions were rushing at me. The use of my first name demoralized me. I sat down.

He set a steaming cup and saucer in front of me and then sat down in a chair across the small, oval table. Absently I noticed that he was using the gold-rimmed, Haviland china which Cousin Della only brought out on special occasions. This indiscretion reinforced what I already knew—this man was a stranger in Della's house. An intruder. Someone who didn't know my cousin well. And yet he seemed to be in command of her kitchen—and of me. Fear as I have never known before overwhelmed me. It made my voice thick, my limbs weak, and the muscles in my stomach tighten as if in a cramp. "What have you done with my Cousin Della?"

"She has met with a slight accident—"

"An accident? What kind of accident? Is she—?"

"She's being taken care of. Your departure tomorrow on the Lucania will not be delayed because of it. Arrangements have been made for me to accompany you."

He had said it again. I had not been mistaken. My trembling hands clenched into tight fists. "I don't know who you are but you presume too much, sir. Nothing . . . nothing would persuade me to accept your company in this . . . or any other situation."

He leaned back in the cane chair, his eyes lazily accessing my flaming face, traveling from the wisps of chestnut hair springing lightly on my forehead, to the flaring nostrils of my slender nose and a full mouth now drawn in a haughty, tight line. Rather than reacting to the hostility oozing from every pore of my body, he seemed amused by it . . . and perhaps even regarded it with grudging admiration. I knew then that he had been prepared for feminine vapors—he probably had smelling salts handy. He took a sip of his tea with delicate slowness . . . as if there were all the time in the world to discuss the preposterous statement he had made. "Drink your tea—" he insisted.

"Where is Cousin Della?" My voice rose more than I would have liked. Anger overrode some of my fear. I would show him that he had no whimpering, pliable female on his hands.

"In a place where she is being cared for . . . You don't need to worry about her. She knows you will be departing tomorrow without her. She is aware of your new companion."

"You're insane!" Tea sloshed out of the cup

as I set it down with a thump. I rose to my feet and clumsily knocked against the table, spilling some of his. "I'm going to the police."

I spun around, expecting him to lunge forward and try to restrain me, but he just sat there, like a poised forest beast sure of his prey. Before I reached the hall doorway, he said in a firm, unhurried voice, "Not if you care about the welfare of your father, Charlotte. It would be a shame if something happened to Professor Conrad because of a foolish action on your part."

He could not have halted my flight any more securely with a deft lasso than he had with those words. My father . . . The man's cold, deadly tone held a promise. I knew he was not bluffing. Thoughts tumbled in a mental whirlwind and immobilzed me . . . Cousin Della had been hurt and taken away . . . perhaps even killed. The man was spewing lies about her being all right. Was my father in the same kind of danger? I couldn't chance it . . . not until I knew more.

"Sit down . . . and finish your tea."

I came back to the table. My weak knees dropped me onto the chair.

"That's better," he said in an infuriatingly patronizing tone. "Try to relax . . . you're not in any danger, Charlotte."

I glared at him across the table. His eyes were slightly shuttered and I knew that behind those half-closed lids, those gray eyes were watching every flicker of my lashes and analyzing every dry swallow in my throat. I had never been one for lukewarm emotions and at that moment I felt such over-whelming hatred that adrenaline flowed through my veins like firewater. His reassurance that I was in no danger only inflamed the raging fury within me. It was all I could do not to fly at him with my nails bared. I knew my only hope lay in controlling my emotions. So I said as evenly as I could, "Cousin Della has been hurt. . . . My father is in danger—"

"Only if you refuse to do a very simple thing —go ahead with your scheduled passage tomorrow. It's as simple as that."

He was lying. Nothing about this bizarre situation was simple. I would need all the acuity I could muster to play his game until I could determine the right moment to thwart him. "But I don't understand," I said in what I hoped was a placating, weak tone. I was not practiced in feminine arts and I feared my fiery eyes did not match my suddenly docile attitude.

"You don't have to understand," he answered bluntly, unmoved by the half-flutter of my eye-lashes. "The plans for your journey have all been made—"

"Yes, but I couldn't travel alone—an unchaperoned young woman—"

"I told you I'm going with you."

Horrified, I dropped my placating manner. How dare he! Did he intend to make me a harlot, a fancy woman? No respectable, unmarried woman would travel alone in a man's company. The degradation would be unbearable. I could never show my face in respectable company again. He couldn't make me do it! And then I remembered his threat against my father. Was this the price I must pay to this horrible man? No, he couldn't force me! "That's impossible," I flared. "Improper, scandalous—"

"Not really . . . not if we were married."

I couldn't move. This stranger smiling at me as he sipped his tea blurred in my vision. The moment had no reality. I was living a macabre nightmare. "Married." The word was like a devastating physical blow to my head and I reeled from it.

He said almost apologetically, "I wish there were some other way, Charlotte, but society being what it is, marriage is the only answer. I have to go with you on this trip and a honeymoon seems an appropriate and satisfying arrangement."

"No!"

"I have no designs upon your person, Miss Conrad. Believe me, our relationship will be platonic . . . except in the eyes of those around us. A legal certificate of marriage is important so—" He gave a helpless gesture of his hands. "I'm afraid I have to insist on an authentic ceremony . . . tomorrow . . . before we embark."

"You're insane!"

He shrugged.

"And if . . . if I refuse?"

"You won't. There will be someone with Professor Conrad constantly until we are aboard the Lucania as man and wife. If you refuse to cooperate—" he shrugged. His mouth was expressive and mobile and at the moment his lips were drawn in a granite hardness that resembled chipped stone.

A legal ceremony . . . tomorrow . . . before we embark. Some detached part of my mind struggled to comprehend his words. Nothing in this stranger's wintry expression showed any signs of weakness nor indecision. *He was going to force me to marry him.* I knew that he was prepared to sweep aside as irrelevant any protests I might make but I could not still my indignation.

"I would never marry you! Never!"

His steady gaze never left my flushed face. "Yes, you will. You love your father. You would not willingly bring any harm upon his head."

I wanted to fling the confident words back down his throat, but I couldn't. What he said was true. I loved my father. There was no one else in my rather drab, uneventful life. Just the two of us. Some people had criticized my father for keeping me so closely confined, but I didn't mind. He was a very entertaining, intelligent companion and I much preferred his company to any of the young swains who visited our home. I did not resent his overprotective attitude. There was nothing I wouldn't do to insure his happiness. Apparently this diabolical stranger knew me all too well. In fact, he even seemed to read my thoughts. "You'll protect your father," he said with infuriating calmness. "You've always been a very dutiful daughter."

"How do you know?" I gasped, suddenly feeling vulnerable and exposed.

His answer confirmed my fears. "I've made it my business to know you very well. You are a devoted daughter who will not put her father's welfare in any kind of jeopardy. That's true, isn't it?"

I wanted to shout that he had misjudged me ... that I was walking out of my cousin's house and going straight to the police. The impulse to defy him was so great that it was all I could do to control it. My hands knotted together in my lap. I looked straight at him. "How do I know ... that my father will be safe—?"

"You can trust me."

Hysterical laughter caught in my throat. *Trust!* He had kidnapped my cousin Della and maybe killed her, threatened the life of my father and intended to force me into a hostage marriage! How could he sit there calmly and talk about trust?

"You don't have any choice, Charlotte."

I knew then that he didn't care whether or not I trusted him. He was in control. No matter how I longed to defy him, I would never put my father in danger. If I didn't cooperate, he would inform his accomplice and something would happen to him. "Don't insult me with any prattle about trust!" I flung at him. "And I swear to you, if any harm comes to my father, I'll see you hanged!"

"Fair enough." He nodded in agreement as if some pact had been made between us.

I choked with fury as he calmly took another sip of tea. It seemed to me that some of the muscular tension had eased from the smooth skin molding his cheekbones and bold chin. My lack of hysterics had undoubtedly been a relief to him. Perhaps I had already lulled him into a false sense of security, I thought with a spurt of hope. That seemed to be the wisest course of action at the moment, play along with him and wait for that moment when I could extricate myself from this monstrous situation. Yes, I must find out everything I could. The whole diabolical scheme obviously had been well planned, carefully timed. If I could get him to talk, he might give me some clue as to how I could thwart his insane demands.

I leaned back in my chair and took a sip of tea. "It's not going to work," I said evenly. "You can't just abduct me. It's impossible to carry of something as preposterous as this 'pretend' honeymoon."

"Not at all. Everything has been taken care of. . . . It has been since you boarded the train in Philadelphia."

His words brought back my uneasiness at the station . . . the cold prickling on my neck. "You . . . you watched me . . . on the train . . . at the station . . . and arranged to get here before me."

He nodded and then had the audacity to smile.

"You paid the driver to take the long way," I

said, aghast at the careful manipulation of events. If only I had trusted my intuition! "I thought the driver was trying to abduct me!"

"I'm sorry to have put you through any undue anxiety," he said with measured politeness.

"You even arranged for me to come alone, didn't you?"

He nodded, watching the bewilderment that swept up into my face. I swallowed back a new wash of fear. The extent of his unscrupulous power was terrifying. This stranger had arranged for my father's colleague to become ill so my father could not accompany me! The enormity of the deceit was overwhelming. He was not acting alone. Other people were involved. It was a conspiracy. A terrifying conspiracy. And none of it made sense. Why were my father, my cousin, and myself being manipulated like important pawns in some sinister game?

"Everything went as planned," he said with obvious satisfaction.

"I knew someone was watching me at the station," I flung at him. "I felt it!"

"Very perceptive—" He nodded approvingly and his lips curved slightly. "You forced me to be very cautious. I didn't want you to know that I was dogging your footsteps."

"If I had noticed you," I spat, "you might be in jail this very minute." I lifted my chin, making no attempt to disguise the joy that such a possibility brought me.

"You did just what we hoped you would—"

I became defensive. "I thought my cousin had just been delayed . . . and so I came directly here. I had no way of knowing someone was intent upon drawing me into such madness." My voice was strangely calm, as if we were about to discuss some rational project instead of a diabolical scheme bringing disaster to everyone I loved. "Why are you doing this?"

He stood up, took away my cup and poured out the cold tea. As he stood with his back to me, I was aware of the breadth of his shoulders and the hard sinews of muscles rippling in his torso. A vague trail of fear slithered up my back. There was a masculine grace to his movements that was almost feline. His hands were large and dexterous, like tiger's paws. I was mesmerized by those hands as he brought a matching teapot to the table and poured me another cup. "Don't let this one get cold," he ordered.

My back stiffened but I knew I must play along with him, learn all I could . . . and then strike back to defeat him. A cup of hot tea might help keep my wits about me. I raised the steaming liquid to my cold, trembling lips.

"That's better. Now, I'll tell you what's going to happen . . . but not *why*. That need not concern you. Tomorrow morning, there will be a short wedding ceremony here, in your cousin's parlor. Then we will leave on our honeymoon—"

Once more I gasped a violent "No!" but he ignored my automatic protest. "Arrangements have already been made for a change in accommodations on the Lucania . . . the kind which will set your mind at ease, I trust . . . two bedrooms with a sitting room between, a kind of neutral zone, if you wish." His eyes seemed about to soften and I saw a hint of smoky blue around the black pupils. Then the flicker was gone and that icy pewter gray made me think I had been mistaken.

"You can't get away with it."

"Oh, yes, I think we can . . . with your cooperation."

"Why me . . . why not someone else?" It was probably a selfish reaction, but it was ribbed with involuntary curiosity.

"You're the only woman in the whole wide world exactly right, Charlotte Lynne Conrad."

"Right . . . For what?"

His lips curved as if appreciating my quick thrust. "To be my bride." He knew my middle name—and how many more intimate details? I felt exposed . . . as if everything personal about me had undergone his scrutiny. "What if I had decided not to come—?" I countered, knowing my eyes were flashing with the rage building within.

"But you did . . . and that's all we have to deal with, for the moment."

"You can't get away with it; my father will surely find out about everything—"

"Perhaps . . . but not immediately . . . and that's what is vital to success. We'll be on that ship tomorrow, Charlotte—as man and wife."

"Maybe I'll refuse—"

"You're a loving daughter . . . and you're not going to do anything that will jeopardize your father's welfare," he countered with infuriating confidence.

"How do you know? I just might call your bluff."

His lazy, catlike glance once more lingered on my face, stroking it with the deliberateness of a languid caress. He said softly, "I know you very well, Charlotte," and reached out and took my hand.

The action was so quick and unexpected that for a moment I couldn't move. His intimate tone brought color rushing hotly up into my cheeks. He held my eyes and managed to make me feel naked before his bold gaze. I was bewildered by an emotion besides anger which suddenly caught in my throat. I did not want to react to him in any way, certainly not as a man. I was horrified as sexual tension suddenly ignited between us. It was impossible! I hated this stranger . . . and yet his touch was sending warmth spiraling through my flesh. "You're the devil," I gasped, jerking my hand away.

I heard his laughter then. For a moment I shut my eyes tightly and stiffened against the sound. Then his mirth stopped as quickly as it had begun and when I opened my eyes, his chair was empty. My head swung around.

"I'll take your things upstairs," he said from

the kitchen doorway behind me. "You'll want a bit to eat later and a good night's sleep. I knew from the moment I saw you, Charlotte, that you were going to make a beautiful bride."

3

The wind kept up its thrashing, wailing and lamenting most of the night. A relentless peppering of rain against the window worked on my frayed nerves. I lay rigid and awake, staring unseen at the ceiling and heard the big grandfather clock on the landing chime two o'clock. There was a funny, bitter taste in my mouth and I wondered if the tea had been drugged. He had urged me to drink it but I was glad that I had only sipped a little of it. If he had expected me to sleep away the hours until morning, I was determined to thwart him.

I was in the upstairs bedroom which I always had when visiting Cousin Della. The lovely white furniture, the pretty walls papered in shades of spring green and pink, and a recessed window seat had made it my favorite room in the house. I had spent many hours sitting in the window, looking out at the small walled garden and dreaming a young girl's fancies. Those memories seemed a mockery now. The saturnine man whom I had left downstairs at the table had destroyed them all. I was caught in a treacherous net that could destroy everything I had ever dreamed about. My thought was that once I had served his purpose, he would callously toss me aside. Every hour brought me closer to disaster.

My mind worked at a frantic pace. Like someone turning on a bed of nettles, I tried to find a way out of the torturous situation. The memory of Della's luggage and hatbox sitting abandoned in the hall was a poignant reminder that she had been whisked away in the middle of her preparations for our trip. Where was she? An accident, my captor had said. That could mean anything. Sometimes death was referred to as a "tragic accident". I could not believe that she wasn't here, in her house, enjoying her lovely things, filling each room with her sweet jasmine perfume. But she was gone. Taken away. Where? And why? My mind was weary with sorting, and speculating.

As the grandfather clock chimed each quarter hour, I could not lie there meekly and accept a stranger's dictates about something that could ruin my whole life. Without knowing exactly what I intended to do, I slipped out of bed and buttoned up my soft pale yellow robe. Walking barefooted, I quietly tiptoed across the room to the door. I turned the knob. It was unlocked. My captor must have thought the tea would keep me drugged until morning. No wonder he had been so insistent that I drink it.

For a moment, I hesitated in the open doorway. I wondered if I should get dressed and try to escape from the house. Once outside in the darkness and the rain I could probably get away. I was tempted but one thought held me back. What if my escape triggered the harm which he had promised awaited my father if I didn't cooperate? He had made it clear that I must cooperate to keep my father from harm. No, I couldn't chance it—but I could try to find out exactly what had happened to my aunt. Perhaps the knowledge would help me thwart the man's evil designs.

I eased out into the dim hall, listening and waiting for some sound that would tell me if my jailer were asleep in one of the bedrooms or waiting downstairs. Nothing. Only the sounds of a house shifting at night and the loud ticking of the grandfather clock.

Cousin Della had left her hatbox and suitcase in the foyer—that meant she had been interrupted in her preparations to meet me. She must have been downstairs, perhaps in her small library or the sitting parlor. If she had been forcibly taken away, some sign of it might remain. I might discover whether or not she had been lured from the house under some false pretense. Or I might find absolutely nothing . . . but even that would be better than lying in bed, waiting for the net to tighten around me tomorrow, I thought as I moved forward along the landing, putting a guiding hand upon the smooth banister.

I was glad I knew the house well enough to quietly navigate the hall and stairs in the dark shadows of the unlighted house. I feared the slightest sound would alert the stranger, wherever he was. Pressed against the wall, I slowly descended, stopping for a moment on each carpeted stair. The loud, measured tick-tock of the tall clock was reassuring and when I reached the landing, I peered over the balcony, tensely waiting to see some movement in the dappled shadows. Only the clock and the loud thumping of my heart disturbed the night as I assured myself it was safe to descend the rest of the stairs.

Because I had already been in the sitting room and had seen nothing to advise me of Cousin Della's fate, I decided to try the library first. I held my breath and crossed the hall to the paneled room where Cousin Della often sat in front of an exquisite escritoire to write letters. The walls were lined with books that had been her husband's and I knew that she kept them more for his memory than any love of reading.

The darkened room was illuminated by the muted light of a street lamp shining through the drizzle of rain outside. As quietly as I could I closed the hall door and turned on a small hurricane lamp. I put my fists against my mouth to stifle a cry. My cousin's small lady's chair which always sat in front of her desk had been turned over—as if she had been jerked out of it or upset it in her haste.

I frantically searched the top of the desk. Her ebony pen which usually rested in a lovely ceramic holder lay flat on her desk with black ink left upon the pen point. She must have been writing when something or someone had disturbed her. As always, everything else was in its place. My Cousin kept a meticulous desk. Anyone who did not know Cousin Della's meticulous ways would have missed the sheet of uneven stationery in one of the pigeonholes of the desk. My eyes fixed on it. It looked as if she had hastily stuck it there. It was as if her spirit had guided me downstairs to find it. I drew it out and was not surprised to see a half-finished note with my name on it. I held my breath as I read it.

"Dearest Charlotte, I am sending this by messenger to intercept you at the depot. Do not come to the house! I cannot explain but you and your father must be kept out of this. Please go back home as quickly as possible. I do not want it on my conscience that I have brought harm upon your heads. If you care about your father and about me, you will—"

The writing broke off there. She must have been interrupted and shoved the unfinished note into the pigeonhole. Something or someone had prevented her from sending it to the station to warn me. I had found her message, but it was too late. "If you care about your father and about me, you will—" The words were a diabolical chant in my ears. Tears flooded my eyes. I had found her message but it only reinforced the stranger's demands.

All the fight went out of me then. I went back upstairs and cried into my pillow. The discovery of my cousin's note had only embedded me in the situation even more than I had been before. Her warning was almost a personal directive not to jeopardize her or my father's welfare.

In a few hours I would stand beside a stranger in Cousin Della's charming parlor and become a hostage bride to a detested man I didn't even know. What if I refused to say the vows necesary to unite us as man and wife? What if I decided to glare mutely at him, refusing to mouth the marriage vows? What would the horrid man do then? I could imagine the coldness of those pewter gray eyes washing over me and I could not stifle an involuntary shudder. Whatever drove this man, it was a commitment that was ribbed with iron determination. I knew that he was not alone in this fiendish abduction. Even if I managed to thwart him, I was certain there were others who might not be manipulated. I could sense power and impersonal dedication behind whatever was going on. How could I put my father's life in jeopardy? The stranger had already demonstrated that "they" could remove people from my life. Cousin Della? How could I believe that she was safe when everything pointed to the contrary? She had been removed so that I would be alone and vulnerable. How permanent her removal had been, I couldn't bear to think. How could I test my captor's threats against my father by refusing to do as he said?

It wasn't my own safety that kept my heart thumping under my rib cage as I struggled to make sense of the appalling events ahead of me. I loved my father dearly. Because my mother had died during my adolescent years, the bond between us was even stronger than that between most fathers and daughters. Our house near the University had become a center of activity and I gladly played the role of hostess, secretary, companion and, at times, mentor to my beloved parent. I had been completely happy until my nineteenth birthday when an insidious discontent had begun to make me restless like a young filly straining at a harness. I realized now that I should have been content with my well-ordered life. This present upheaval mocked my restlessness. Sometimes life gives us what we want, I thought, and then we find that all those things we have taken for granted are precious indeed. None of the male visitors to our house attracted me as suitors and even Randell Delany's attentions had worn thin. Now as I lay there, caught in a mesh of deception, I wished I had been less critical of Randell. I had found him a little tedious, engrossed in his duties as assistant professor in the social science department, and I had refused his proposal of marriage because it seemed to offer little more than I already had in my life.

I had never thought myself overly sentimental but as I visualized my marriage to a detested stranger, tears spilled hotly down my cheeks. I didn't even know the man's name. Soon I would be Mrs. Something-or-Other, wearing a wedding band and departing on my honeymoon with a horrid man who was determined to cruelly manipulate me as he saw fit.

Although I had battered him with questions before I had haughtily removed myself to go upstairs the evening before, I had learned little. He gave every indication that his diabolical scheme would continue once we reached England if he still had need of me. What that need would be, I could not fathom but I clenched my fists and vowed that before the Lucania docked, any such plan would be thwarted.

I had never been of a temperament that accepted a man's domination. My education had been liberal and I had participated in many academic discussions beyond the scope of most women. To cooperate blindly in this elaborate intrigue without using every dram of acuity I possessed to discern his motives was contrary to my nature. At the moment he seemed to have a halter around my neck leading me where he chose but he would not be able to control everything in the environment. Something in his plan was bound to go amiss. I had to be prepared for that moment . . . and seize it.

I didn't fall asleep until the first wash of gray dawn was seeping around the edges of the window shutters and then it seemed only moments later that I heard footsteps in the hall.

There was a light tap at my door. "Charlotte?" His voice was as I remembered, controlled, hard like chipped marble, and it caused a prickling of fear to ease up my spine. I closed my eyes and refused to answer. Perhaps I had foolishly hoped that by morning, he would be gone . . . and yesterday's events would have truly been a nightmare. Now, reality swept back with fresh horror and greater intensity. "Charlotte," he repeated. "Here's a breakfast tray. . . . The minister will be here in an hour. Please come down when you're ready."

I wanted to scream at him that I was never coming down but I knew that my only escape from this madness was to feign a placid and frightened acceptance of his orders. And when the right moment came, I would see him crushed and that quiet arrogance shattered.

This thought goaded me as I performed my toilette and took out the new forest green traveling suit I had brought in the portmanteau to wear for our departure. Now it would be my wedding gown. The pain of this thought was unbearable until I reminded myself that the ceremony would be an empty ritual, having no meaning now or ever.

I made no attempt to do anything fancy with

my thick russet hair. In fact, I took some pleasure in trying to make it smooth and unadorned although it's natural curliness defeated me. Tiny wisps of auburn hair curled softly on my forehead and trailed over my ears. With the deftness of a chameleon my hazel eyes reflected the color of my attire and this morning they deepened with the dark green hue of my velvet hat and gown. They looked back at me from the reflection in the mirror. Wide, heavily lashed eyes were my best feature but at the moment they were only windows that showed the agitation and fright I felt inside.

I managed to eat the toast and fruit, and drink the tea he had left on the tray outside my door. Since I had refused to eat anything last night, my empty stomach grumbled thankfully as I forced down the food. I knew I must keep up my strength. If I allowed myself to become weak, either physically or mentally, I would not be able to seize the opportunity to take control of the situation. My granite-eyed tormentor was human; he had to have his own Achilles' heel—and I intended to find it! I had just finished as the sound of the door knocker floated up the stairs and reached my ears with all the connotations of a death knell. Someone was at the front door.

The Minister? It must be. The marriage would take place in Della's parlor. I wanted to cry. That lovely room was very special to me. My father and I had enjoyed holiday festivities, birthday celebrations, and other special occasions there—and now it was to be the setting for my wedding.

In a moment my abductor would be at the bedroom door to escort me down to the parlor like a condemned prisoner, forcibly, if necessary. I straightened my shoulders. My foolish pride insisted on more dignity than being led like a lamb to the proverbial slaughter. I would do what he said. I would go downstairs with my chin high and my back straight and with every sense alerted to crush him the first moment possible.

I gave one last look around the room, like someone trying to hoard the warmth and familiarity of each object against some future emotional famine. Last night's storm had moved on. An eager sun was shining down upon grass and leaves which sparkled with dazzling brightness. "Happy the bride, the sun shines on." The aphorism was painful. I wondered if I would ever see this house again. As I looked out the window at the small, landscaped rose garden where I had spent so many contented hours in the garden swing, I felt like someone about to take a step off a terrifying precipice—only a miracle could save me from disaster.

Blinking against a sudden fullness in my eyes, I turned away from the window. There was no sense in torturing myself with such nostalgic thoughts. I must not look back but concentrate on the present, I schooled myself. This was no time to feel sorry for myself. The strength I needed would come from marshaling my wits against the man waiting for me downstairs.

I went out into the hall, and haughtily descended the steps. Despite my determination not to show my inner trepidation, my steps faltered as I neared the bottom.

Standing to one side of the staircase near the carved newel post, he was only a shadow for a moment, a gray, waiting specter. Then he stepped forward.

I froze as he offered his hand to guide me down the few remaining steps. His face was touched with sunlight coming through the tinted rose window and for a second there was a gentleness there, a hint of understanding and empathy. I foolishly reached out for it. "Please . . . please don't do this." I even held on to his hand which engulfed mine as I descended the last step and reached his side.

For a moment I had the illusion that he could not be the devil of yesterday. His well-chiseled features carried a handsomeness that I had missed during my emotional upheaval. The black suit was gone and he wore a stylish frock coat in dark maroon which matched gray and maroon striped trousers. His white linen was impeccable and set off by a brocade vest and soft black tie. His gray eyes seemed less formidable and for a brief instant I thought he was going to say the words I wanted to hear.

I held my breath as his eyes narrowed and his hand squeezed mine. Then the hope that had sprung into my chest quickly dissolved.

"Reverend Dingham and the witnesses are waiting," he said. His tone lacked any softness or warmth. He drew me forward across the polished hall floor into the front parlor.

I had never felt such hate. It consumed me. I knew then I could not depend upon his definition of this marriage. He would take from it what he wished, and in the eyes of the law I would be his chattel.

Cousin Della's lovely parlor became a setting for a nightmare. I felt detached from my own body, like someone watching the unbelievable scenario from a distance. Two elderly women bobbed their gray heads with approval as we took our places. A paunchy, bald-headed man stood in front of the fireplace. He looked slightly bleary-eyed as he began to read the service in a monotone. "We are gathered here today to join Adam Demorest and Charlotte Conrad in holy matrimony."

Adam Demorest. Was that his real name . . . or was it a sham like everything else about him? He spoke his vows in a firm even tone, and I felt those fathomless wintry eyes boring into my pale face. I was suspended in some kind of floating limbo, part of the scene and yet detached from it. As he stood beside me and slipped a ring on my finger with alacrity, he had no substance or reality.

The simple words, "I do" stuck in my throat but the fat preacher with beads of sweat on his speckled head took the strangled sound as affirmation of my vows. Only the phrase "Till death do us part" rang in my ears with diabolical insistence, like the vibration of a tuning fork, as if some facet of my mind knew the marital promise to be a poignant warning.

"I now pronounce you man and wife. You may kiss the bride."

In my detached limbo, I didn't react. His arm encircled my waist and with bewildering swiftness, he laid his lips on mine. The suddenness of the contact did not allow me time to summon my defenses. Before I could make my mouth rigid, his kiss found a soft yielding that I sought to deny. I willed a refusal, a frigid coldness to my lips that was not there. It was a brief contact . . . but a shattering one. He lifted his mouth and for a moment those narrowed eyes held mine. I must have trembled for he murmured, "Steady."

A certificate of marriage was placed on a nearby French provincial table and we affixed our names to it. It seemed to be an authentic marriage license with all the proper signatures and disproved my suspicions that the marriage ceremony might have been a sham. No, it had been a legal marriage and my heart sank as my lawful husband turned smoothly away. He thanked the tittering ladies, and put an envelope into the pudgy hand of the preacher.

I sat down on the edge of Cousin Della's brocaded parlor chair like one in shock while he saw them out. The muted colors in her Aubusson carpet and the heavy oyster-white draperies with their gold cords and tassels mocked me as I looked about. Cousin Della's priceless vases and Dresden china figures were as familiar as my own tiny watch pinned on my lapel but I was disoriented. The same relentless words kept going through my mind, "This isn't happening . . . this isn't happening—"

An instinct for self-preservation urged me to flee but a stronger rationality that defied interpretation kept me sitting there. I heard the outside door close, the murmur of voices float away; the house was suddenly enveloped in a possessive stillness. Like one unable to function because of shock, I just sat there.

"You did very well," he said when he came back and picked up the marriage license. "I promise you, Charlotte, that you won't be sorry."

My head came up. "And I promise *you*, sir, that you will be!" My ready temper poured warmth back into my iced veins.

The vindictiveness in my voice seemed to startle him and I could see the muscles in his lean cheeks tighten visibly. The room crackled with an emotional charge. It was pure idiocy to taunt him.

He folded up the certificate and put it in the inside pocket of his coat without taking his gaze from my face. "I don't expect you to understand—"

Foolish tears filled my eyes then. "I understand perfectly well . . . I have just been legally married to a man whom I abhor . . . who is so despicable I feel myself capable of murder."

A slight quirk at the corner of his mouth mocked my outburst. "Then I shall have to make certain I sleep with one eye open. And now my dear wife—"

"I am not your wife!"

A flash of anger glinted in those steel gray eyes. "Yes, you are . . . and you'd better act as such when we are out in public. When we are alone you can vent all the anger you wish . . . but from this moment on you are Mrs. Adam Demorest . . . and you'd better start calling me Adam, instead of sir."

"Yes, sir," I snapped. "Very good, sir. Whatever you say, sir!"

"You little—" He jerked me to my feet. I thought he was going to hit me but instead he bent his head. *He was going to kiss me.* This time enough fury flowed through my body that I angrily jerked my mouth away and braced my hands against his chest. With a deft, smooth movement, he pinned my arms at my side, and held me captive against him. He buried his face in the nape of my neck. The searing warmth of his lips touched my skin in an intimate kiss and he ordered, "Now say it . . . Adam."

"Let me go!" I gasped. My senses were reeling with this unexpected assault. No man had ever held me in such an embrace. My physical response defied inhibitions and conditioning as he trailed light kisses up my neck. "Adam," he whispered. "Say it."

"No."

His lips moved in butterfly kisses across my

cheek until they touched the corner of my mouth. "Adam, say it . . . unless you want to be persuaded further—?"

The threat brought me back to my senses. "Adam!" I spat as if the name were something foul.

"Again . . . softer—"

"Adam . . . Adam . . . Adam—" My voice was strident.

"Not quite right . . . try again." His lips moved in butterfly kisses around my mouth, lightly releasing a rush of bewildering sensation at his touch.

I gasped like one searching for air. "Adam," I gasped, my senses tingling from lips softly tasting the corners of my mouth. "Please . . . let . . . me go . . . Adam." My voice was strangely husky.

"That's better." His embrace tightened for a moment and then he dropped his arms, freeing me from the circle of his embrace. I let myself drop back down into the chair, struggling with emotions that were reeling away like wild horses at the end of a dozen reins.

He gave me a moment to compose myself and then he said with unbelievable calmness. "I have hired a carriage to take us to the pier. It will be here shortly. I'm sure you would like to freshen up. By the way, there is a corsage in the hall. Please fasten it to your dress, and be prepared for some fuss on the ship over the newlyweds on their honeymoon—"

It wasn't over. The wedding was only the

beginning.

"Don't look like that! Those wide, sea-green eyes of yours betray your every thought. Now listen to me. Once we leave this house, your performance will have to be convincing." He clenched his hands and I thought he might reach out and shake my shoulders. "You are Mrs. Adam Demorest—a brand-new bride on her honeymoon. I have made some notes for you to memorize and, believe me, you'd better be convincing or—" he faltered.

"Or you will harm my father! Why don't you say it? Your threats are plain enough to understand. I'm a puppet hostage, forced to talk and act according to the vicious strings you pull. No telling what you will expect me to do."

"Nothing more than I've said. Believe me, Charlotte, all you have to do is play the part of a happy bride on her honeymoon—"

"How can you expect me to do that when—"

"When you dislike me?"

"Dislike?" I gasped. "I despise you . . . loathe you . . . abhor being in the same room with you. I—"

"That's enough!" His voice was like the snap of a whip. "Go upstairs and collect your things. The carriage will be here shortly. And remember . . . the personal feelings between you and me are not important. There is something more important at stake here. And you have your father's welfare to think of. I suggest that you not forget that important fact when you are indulging in your abhorrence of me."

"How will I know papa's all right—?" I parried.

"If things have gone well, you can send him a cablegram when we reach England to confirm it."

"And Cousin Della?" I pressed.

"I told you—it was necessary to remove her from the situation."

His ominous words floated in the air like poisonous motes. I was convinced then that he had killed her.

4

I threw an anguished look back at Cousin Della's brownstone house as I sat stiffly in the hansom cab beside my captor-husband. Would I ever see it again? Somehow there was a finality in the crack of the driver's whip as the horse lurched away from the curbing. The sound echoed in my mind as an end to everything in my life that had been sane and ordered.

There was very little that I could read in the expression of the man sitting next to me. A slight pulling of his dark eyebrows hinted that his thoughts were not as tranquil as the smooth lines of his cheeks and mouth. He wore a tall black hat and leather gloves. He had put a white boutonniere in the coat he wore like a cape over his frock coat and striped trousers. He turned to look at me and I jerked my eyes away.

The warmth of his kisses still tingled on my

skin. I was furious with myself for having given in to his demand to speak his name softly. The sensation of those lips tracing the soft valleys of my neck and cheeks and circling my mouth with tantalizing persuasion had defeated my anger. But it wouldn't happen again, I swore silently, staring blankly out the carriage window. Somehow I had lost the first battle. I had allowed him to take possession of my emotions. The sweet perfume of the double gardenia corsage pinned to my bodice was sickening and I wanted to jerk it off and let the horses in the New York streets trample it underfoot.

There were people everywhere, jostling with carriages and huge drays and workhorses, and pushing through carts lined up along the curbing. I thought about jerking open the carriage door and fleeing into the crowd but such impulsive action would be pure folly. I was as securely tied to the man sitting beside me as a trained bear was to his master. One jerk on the string and I had to obey. I could not even scream at the mounted policemen riding by my window. One young redheaded officer even tipped his hat and smiled at me as we passed his corner and I was helpless to do anything but give him a feeble smile back.

I jumped when my warden touched my arm. My head swung around and I knew that my eyes were filled with the rage I felt. He ignored my reaction and handed me several sheets of paper filled with solid writing. "Here are some details which I want you to memorize before we reach the ship."

I looked at the number of pages. "But that's impossible!"

"No, it isn't. Not for you, Charlotte. You have a quick memory and almost total recall. Your record at Wynburn Women's College was outstanding . . . and it was due in part to your ability to quickly assimilate empirical information."

I knew my mouth had dropped open. "How . . . do you know that?"

"I made it my business to find out everything I could about you before . . . before selecting you as my bride. It was important to have the right person."

"I'm flattered," I said sarcastically. "I wouldn't have wanted to fail any tests for qualifying as your hostage."

He smiled then. It was the first time I had seen a feather of smoky blue soften his eyes. The effect was startling. I had to look away quickly to the sheets of paper clutched in my gloved hand in order to keep from responding to a charm that was as deadly as an elusive snake. My first instinct was to shove the papers away and tell him haughtily that he'd gotten the wrong bride after all. Perhaps it was curiosity, or lingering fright, or a flash of common sense that made me read through the material.

"Adam Demorest . . . age thirty . . . parents deceased . . . occupation, lawyer . . . graduate of

Harvard Law School. Business address: Colter Building, New York City. Parents dead, one brother living in Boston—" I looked up after I'd finished the first sheet. "All fabricated lies, I assume."

"No. The first page is mostly fact . . . with a considerable number of omissions . . . the rest of the material is fiction," he said sociably as if we were discussing some literary work.

"Like whether or not you're married."

"Oh, I'm married . . . to you. I'm not a bigamist, Charlotte."

"That might be the kindest thing that could be said about you," I retorted.

He smiled again and I knew my insults only amused him.

I turned to the second sheet. "Romance with Charlotte Conrad began during an educational conference in Philadelphia last fall." With utter amazement I read the complete scenario which followed delineating a courtship that never happened. It was unbelievable! The last six months of my life had been carefully scrutinized and the fabricated romance deftly interwoven with actual events and people. It appalled me to think that I had been under such close surveillance. A record of people and events was there, detailed and accurate. Anyone not knowing the truth could have been persuaded that a short engagement and surprise marriage could have happened the way it was related on those pages. Only it hadn't!

Everything written there was a mesh of fabricated deceit.

"I'll fill out more background as the situation warrants," he said.

"I'm not a good liar. I can't parrot these lies . . . pretend they really happened."

"You have to," he responded in a matter-of-fact tone. "People are always curious about newlyweds. They'll be asking questions. Don't volunteer anything but the data that's on those sheets. There'll be no problem if you just convince yourself that what you're saying is the truth."

"The truth! I would love to tell them the truth! That my cousin may be in danger of her life . . . and that you blackmailed me into marrying you. I don't know if you are using your real name or if any of the facts about your background are true. You must think I'm a simpleton to believe anything you say."

"You're no simpleton," he granted. "And you know that at the moment you have no choice but to do as I say."

"That may change," I said with the habitual thrust of my chin.

"Perhaps . . . but I doubt it. Now read. We'll be at the pier in a few minutes."

I read through the material and then handed the papers back to him with a scathing look. "Anything else?" My tone was caustic.

"Yes . . . there may be situations where you need to improvise. It's impossible to cover all the contingencies." His eyes narrowed and his forehead furrowed in a slight frown. "I want you to do a lot of smiling . . . and very little talking."

My spirits rose. He had admitted that there was no way even such careful planning and preparation could be entirely adequate. Some unforeseen development might arise that could trip him up—and I intended to be ready for it.

A few blocks from where the steamer was berthed, we were caught in a bustle of carriages, hacks and wagons, and moved with infuriating slowness toward the water. In spite of the situation, I could not quell a rising excitement as I caught sight of the Lucania. She was the latest passenger steamship to be added to the Cunard Line. The pamphlets Cousin Della had sent me bragged that she was the first vessel to have coal-burning firegrates in all the principal rooms and her accommodations were heralded as "the stately chambers of a palace rather than merely quarters within the steel walls of a ship." I had pored over the brochures until they were frayed and wrinkled from my eager hands. For years I had listened to Cousin Della talk about her travels all over the world and had harbored a secret longing to go with her. Now I was here—and she wasn't.

"I have to know," I pleaded. "Is . . . is Cousin Della dead?"

My questions brought a reaction which I could not identify. Something in his eyes flickered and then faded. "No, of course not.

She's just being . . . detained."

I wanted to believe him. "Are you telling me the truth?"

"Yes." He seemed about ready to say something more. Then he turned away and the moment was lost.

I desperately wanted to believe him.

We alighted from the carriage and Adam made arrangements for the few pieces of luggage which we had with us to be taken aboard and put in the proper staterooms. He took my arm and guided me through the milling crowd.

The noise and confusion was that of a loud, bustling carnival. A brass band of six energetic musicians was stationed near the gangplank and blared out martial tunes in a loud and enthusiastic send-off. Bright banners and flags whipped in the breeze atop the ship as people collected on the decks and along the wharf. We almost had to battle our way through the crowd.

The salty air was heavy with humidity from yesterday's rain but the sun managed to peek through and bring an illusion of spring warmth to the dock. Boarding passengers and well-wishers surrounded us, all laughing and chattering, creating a scene I had imagined many times. Now those excited anticipations of my first journey abroad were a mockery to the leaden spirits with which I mounted the gangplank, wearing a gardenia corsage, a detested stranger cupping my elbow.

His lips were slightly curved in a smile as we reached the promenade deck. Adam nodded to a smartly dressed officer who held a passenger list. "Mr. and Mrs. Adam Demorest," Adam said in a clear voice.

The officer's white-toothed smile was practiced as he checked our name off his list. "Welcome aboard, Mr. and Mrs. Demorest."

My secret hope that the officer would find something amiss and see through our charade was not realized. He turned away to greet the next passenger in line.

"Do you want to check out the accommodations first?" my pretend bridegroom asked solicitously, keeping a guiding hand firmly on my arm as he bent his head near mine. "There will be a warning signal for well-wishers to leave the ship and that will be time enough to get to the upper deck to watch the departure."

I nodded. The confusing bustle aboard ship had sapped my courage to defy my abductor. My stomach, already tight with nervousness, did not relax in the confusion of our immediate departure. Already crowds hugged the railing along the promenade decks of the ship, shouting and waving to people who had come to see them off.

We passed into the center of the ship which seemed to me to be larger than most hotel lobbies. The walls were covered with a marble-like wainscoting, huge, fluted pillars rose to a high, embossed ceiling, and a luxurious carpet was spread underfoot, muffling the sound of people mounting broad staircases, coming and going like busy ants. I was grateful for the firm guiding hand on my elbow even as I resented his presence beside me. Immediately I was lost in a catacomb of halls and corridors as we traversed the bowels of the ship.

I hated the closed-in feeling of the narrow corridors with their endless rows of identical doors. I would never be able to find my way to our staterooms. "Do you know where we're going?"

"First-class quarters are midship," he said and I thought I caught an amused quirking at the corner of his lips.

"You've been abroad before, of course," I said sarcastically, knowing that my wide-eyed stare and nervous swallowing was that of an inexperienced ocean traveler.

"Not on the Lucania. She's brand-new. The Cunard Line makes each ship more luxurious than the last. I'm sure you'll be quite comfortable with *our* accommodations."

The pronoun brought back the reality of the moment.

No, it couldn't be. I was trapped in the depths of this ship, as secure as any dungeon, I thought. He had probably lied to me about the privacy of my own cabin. As he opened our stateroom door, I wouldn't have been surprised to see a single room with a double berth. As I stepped inside, he must have heard my sigh of relief.

"I told you that I had engaged a suite."

"Yes, you did but you must forgive me if I don't believe a word you say." I smiled sweetly and swept by him.

Although quite small, the sitting room was fashionably decorated in Victorian style with several upholstered parlor chairs, small tables, and one curved back sofa placed in a comfortable grouping in front of a small fireplace.

The doors on opposite sides of the room must be bedrooms, I thought and chose the doorway on my left. It was as if it had been ordained that I would pick that one. There in the middle of the floor was my steamer trunk that had been sent ahead from Philadelphia nearly a week before. Beside it was my portmanteau—and Cousin Della's suitcase and hatbox. Apparently the hansom driver had thought that they went too. The sight of her things brought back the moment I had opened the door to her house and saw them sitting at the foot of the stairs. Perhaps I knew even then that my cousin had met with foul play. But surely someone would miss her. . . . *Not if everyone thought her away on an extended cruise!*

This truth caught in my throat and my sob was almost inaudible. I knew then that everything had been too carefully arranged to hope that anyone would suspect the diabolical change in plans that had taken place. My father had been deliberately kept in Philadelphia . . . to replace the colleague who had become ill at the last moment. Adam had wanted me to come to

New York alone. He had followed me on the train, arranged for the hack driver to delay in reaching my aunt's house so he could be there first, and then forced me into becoming a hostage for my father's safety. Everything had been deftly and smoothly executed. It was foolish to cling to any hope that authorities would see through the charade and miss my aunt—and rescue me.

There was only my dogged determination to foil his plans. Somehow I would make all this elaborate mesh of treachery for naught. I turned back to the sitting room.

"Everything satisfactory?"

I wanted to laugh at his solicitous tone. "Lovely," I snapped.

"I meant what I said . . . about keeping my distance from you."

"Like you did in the parlor?" I knew I was goading him but I couldn't help myself.

"I'm sorry about that. I shouldn't have lost my temper. You are exasperating, you know. Even now, your eyes are flashing as if you would love to plunge a dagger into my throat."

"And why shouldn't I?"

"Because I don't wish you harm."

"The way you didn't wish Cousin Della harm."

There was a ragged edge to his voice that chilled my blood. "Don't waste your sympathy on her."

How dare he dismiss Cousin Della like that! As if she were of no importance! His ruthless disregard for me and my feelings made me lash out, "How dare you say such a thing! I loved my cousin very much." Only then did I realize I had used the past tense. I bit my underlip to keep from crying.

At that moment a shrill blast of the ship broke the weighted moment. "Come on, let's go on deck," he said, opening the hall door.

"I don't want to!"

"Yes, you do!"

"Why? Because you have some other nefarious scheme for me to carry out?"

"No, because I don't want you to miss the excitement of watching the ship ease away from the wharf and then slowly move down the channel past the Statue of Liberty. It's a sight that you mustn't miss."

I stared at him. Was he telling the truth? What an enigma he was. One moment coldly dismissing the fate of my cousin and the next concerned about my missing a view.

As we left our staterooms, another couple emerged from a doorway across the narrow hall. A rather large woman smiled at us. She was somewhere in her forties, her breasts thrust outward like ripe melons and her large derriere draped with numerous folds of a bustle. She was accompanied by a portly little man who hovered at her side like a tugboat trying to keep her moving. He failed. When she caught sight of us, she stopped in the middle of the corridor and beamed. "Newlyweds. I can tell. And she's as pretty as those flowers she's wearin'. Well, now, I guess we'll have to make sure you two don't stay holed up in your quarters for the whole trip—all that lovin' will save you know.'' She gave a bawdy laugh and gave her husband a knowing slap. "Remember, George, how it was with us.''

"Now, Maudy, you're embarrassing these young folks." His pudgy smile was apologetic. "My wife's an incurable romantic. We've traveled all over the world and she can't resist teasing newlyweds. We're George and Maudy Haversham. Pleased to meet you." He held out his short, fat hand.

Adam's response was crisp and barely polite. "Adam Demorest . . . and my wife, Charlotte."

"Now ain't this nice . . . neighbors and all." The woman smirked and winked at me. "You're looking a little peaked. No need to worry. I'm betting that handsome hubby of yours knows how to make a gal feel real special."

"Maudy!" chastised her husband but she only cackled.

Without giving our fellow travelers a chance to continue the conversation, Adam piloted me past them. I glanced up at him and saw that his profile was as stoney as chipped granite. "What rotten luck," he growled. "Hundreds of people on this boat and we have to have them across the hall." He looked down at me. "I'm sorry . . . I really am." He seemed to be sincere and concerned about my reaction to the woman's crude innuendoes.

"I'm not easily embarrassed," I said honestly.

A few suggestive remarks seemed the least of my worries at the moment.

We emerged on an upper deck but I had no idea of the route we took to get there. Music, people laughing, shouting and throwing streams of confetti to people crowded on the dock below created an exciting bedlam. We found a place at the railing just as a shrill departing whistle signaled that the thirteen-hundred ton steamer was about to slip its moorings. In another few minutes, huge winches began to pull in thick ropes, groaning as they wound them around drumheads. The engines rumbled, and tiny tugboats moved into position. In spite of myself I was caught up in the drama of the moment.

The ship began to move, almost imperceptibly at first, and then the distance grew between us and the dock. A quickening breeze off the water carried a salty smell and the poignant odor of wet hemp and dank wood. We were moving out of New York harbor.

"There she is!" He pointed to the Statue of Liberty. "She's a grand lady, isn't she?"

Once more his expression defied interpretation. Was he pretending some inner stirring of patriotism? Some noble sentiment about leaving the United States? I had to remind myself that he was a master of deceit. I mustn't let his smooth charm blind me to the person that he was. He had forced me into a marriage for some evil design of his own. And my Cousin Della had been his first victim.

I turned my gaze back to the statue and watched it disappear as the Lucania headed out to sea. Deep pangs of homesickness enveloped me. "Let's go below," I said, turning away from the railing.

"All right." He took my arm and then we both froze.

Someone was calling my name. "Charlotte! Charlotte Conrad . . . over here."

I swung around, my heart leaping into my chest.

"It's you, Charlotte Conrad, isn't it?" An elderly gentleman swept off his bowler and smiled at me.

For a moment I couldn't react and then joy burst like spillwater. "Professor Lynwood," I gasped and then laughed joyously. "How wonderful to see you!"

It had happened—the unforeseen complication. Someone aboard knew me! Alexander Lynwood, a dear friend of my father who had been at Oxford with him. I knew that in recent years, Dr. Lynwood had been conducting aerodynamic experiments for the United States government. He had visited us several times in Philadelphia. I flung a triumphant look at Adam Demorest. Then my expression froze. My breath caught and my exuberance instantly withered.

Adam was smiling broadly and holding out his hand to the professor. "How do you do, Professor Lynwood. I'm Adam Demorest. How nice that my wife will be able to enjoy your company on the crossing."

5

I forced my startled gaze away from Adam's face to accept Professor Lynwood's congratulations.

"My dear Charlotte, how wonderful! Newlyweds! And to think we'll be on the same crossing. I haven't seen you for nearly six or seven years. You've grown into a lovely woman." He beamed. His narrow, lean face was dominated by a wide smile. He was a tall man, slightly stooped, with thick bushy gray eyebrows, alert eyes and a mobile expression that defied his sixty years. "What a lovely surprise!"

I reached out and hugged him then. He was someone from the sane world. Someone who knew me! "I'm so glad to see you, Professor Lynwood."

"Oh, my!" He stepped back, obviously a little

embarrassed by my embrace. "You're smashing
your corsage, my dear."

At that moment I wanted to tear it off my
lapel and throw it in the ocean. Here was
someone who could end this vicious charade. A
warning pressure on my arm told me that Adam
had read my thoughts. He said smoothly,
"Charlotte's father will be pleased to learn that
you are on the same crossing, won't he,
darling?"

Her father! It was a firm reminder that his
welfare depended upon her cooperation.

"How is Charles? It seems only yesterday that
we were young men together at Oxford. He was
our fun-loving American . . . and we used to get
into a few scrapes, let me tell you." He laughed
and his face softened with a youthful glow. "I'll
have to tell you some stories about your father.
He's as lively and witty as ever, I'll bet."

"Yes . . . I guess I'm a little homesick
already—" I managed. "It will be nice to talk to
someone who knows him—"

"Perhaps we could join you for dinner—?"
Adam let the sentence hang politely.

"But, of course! I'd be honored. I'm traveling
with my niece and nephew. They would both be
delighted with some young company. I think
they feared I'd collect some old fossils around
me. Won't they be surprised? Newlyweds—my,
my. I bet Professor Conrad is delighted. Are you
also in education, Mr. Demorest?"

"Call me Adam, please, sir. . . . No, I'm a
lawyer. I met Charlotte when I visited Phila-

delphia." Then he went on to recite all the lies I had been told to memorize. As I listened I couldn't find any hesitation or insincerity to label the story as bold lies. It was appalling—and terribly frightening.

Another more perceptive listener might have sensed the lies but Alexander Lynwood was not especially perceptive about people. I knew his life had been spent buried in his work. He had never married, sacrificed everything to work on his conviction that it was possible to create a machine that would fly. His failure to do so had brought harsh condemnation in the press and from his colleagues. The ridicule must have almost destroyed him. He was going back to England as a failure. But he was here—on this ocean liner—when I desperately needed a friend.

I managed a bright smile. "Until tonight, then." My spirits were rising. I wasn't alone. A dear friend of my father was here on the same boat. It wasn't until much later that I began to wonder if he was in the same danger as my Cousin Della.

"Shall we take a short tour around the boat?" asked my solicitous husband after the Professor had disappeared.

I didn't want to go back to our staterooms. Already I had a negative feeling about being trapped down there . . . or imprisoned, as the case might be. I nodded. "Yes, I would like that. It's much bigger than I had imagined."

I wanted to get oriented. I had no intention of

depending upon Adam Demorest to guide me everywhere I wanted to go. The Lucania was a large ship and I intended to put as much of it between me and my captor as often as my wits would allow me to get away from him. Of course, there would be no visible handcuffs but they were there nevertheless. He was going to keep me on a short tether—if he could.

As we walked around the deck and past luxurious rooms designed for indolent travelers, I tried to gain some knowledge of the layout of the ship—which facilities were aft and which were forward. It was true that my memory was excellent but, on the other hand, my instinctive sense of direction was about as poor as it could be. I had to create a visual map in my mind and relate to it instead of relying on clues which my faulty preception gave me. As we walked down wide staircases and lovely wood-panelled corridors, I struggled to draw a blueprint of the ship in my head.

"This is the library. Quite elegant, isn't it?"

"It's beautiful!" I forgot to be tart and withdrawn as I surveyed the elegant, cherry wood paneling and intricately carved beams crisscrossing on the ceiling. Glassed-in bookcases rose to the elaborately embossed moldings of rich, dark polished wood. Lovely lamps were placed in the center of small reading tables. Comfortable swivel chairs fastened to the floor promised hours of comfortable reading. Heavy velvet swags hung at large portholes. They were

the same peacock blue as the upholstered armchairs that lined the room.

I had been raised with books and this room
was reassuring, like an old friend. Many of the
leatherbound volumes were my favorites. I
sighed. "I love to read," I said, and then I
remembered whom I was talking to. "But, of
course, you know that," I added tartly. "No
doubt, you can tell me what books I checked out
of the university library this past winter."

He gave me an enigmatic smile which told me
nothing. "There might be one or two here you
haven't read," he offered, his smile broadening.
"My taste is rather . . . eclectic."

"I don't see any law books," I baited him.
"But, of course, you probably brought your
own—if you really are a lawyer."

"I'm sure I can find something of interest," he
parried.

We circled the room. Polished mahogany
writing desks offered pen and inkwells and
paper imprinted with the Lucania monogram. I
could write my father here . . . but would I be
allowed to post the letter? I raised questioning
eyes to Adam and once more he read my
thoughts.

"Undoubtedly, you'll want to write some
letters."

"And I can post them when we get to port?"

"Of course . . . providing you let me see them
first."

"And if I don't?"

"You will. You are not a foolish girl." His steady gray eyes challenged mine. "I think you understand what I'm saying."

"Perfectly!" I snapped and jerked away.

He did not respond to my display of temper but rather suffered it as one would treat a willful child. I wondered what would happen if I slapped that infuriating calm face of his.

In silence, we continued our tour of the liner.

"Oh, my word!" I gasped. The music room was more dramatic than the library. Gold satin chairs and curved settees accented a long room which was all white and gilt with a white-enamelled grand piano at one end. White pillars, panels, and pilasters provided a lightness that was enhanced by discreet electric lighting in the deep bas-reliefs of the ceiling. "I've never seen anything like it," I breathed, forgetting to be stoic and uncommunicative. The musical soirees given at the college were in heavy, dark rooms which were supposed to match the somber recitals of Bach and Beethoven. "I wonder what kind of musical programs they offer?"

"We'll have to attend some and find out," he said pleasantly.

I knew then that he was never going to let me go anywhere without escorting me. Once more I determined that somehow I was going to thwart my dedicated bridegroom as quickly as possible. I suddenly was quite tired from the emotional demands of the day. I wanted to go in my stateroom and lock the door against him.

When I suggested it, he said, "We'll have some lunch first."

"I'm not hungry."

"You have to eat with me some time, you know," he countered in his unruffled manner. "I promise you that my table manners are quite acceptable. You might even find me to be an adept conversationalist."

"The only thing I find you to be is utterly contemptible."

"Too bad." He gave a mock sigh. "Come along. There's a small restaurant on the upper deck. I think you'll enjoy the view."

I did. And I enjoyed lunch too. In spite of his company.

Wicker and bamboo furniture was placed among lush greenery in the long, narrow restaurant. Colorful pots spilled a rainbow of blossoms to make a Victorian garden in this section of an enclosed deck. Through windows, we could see people circling the ship on the promenade deck.

I scrutinized the passengers and all the diners in the restaurant, hoping that I might see someone else I knew. Adam's reaction to Professor Lynwood had made me uneasy. He obviously thought the older man was no threat to his nefarious schemes.

"See anyone you know?" he asked with that infuriating calmness as he took a bite of lobster.

"I wouldn't tell you if I did."

My tartness did not seem to affect his appetite. Nor his good manners. He obviously had all the social skills needed to order the correct wine for the seafood entrees which he had ordered for both of us. Two obsequious waiters hovered at his elbow as if he were worthy of their attentions.

I had decided I wouldn't give him the pleasure of seeing me eat but when the aromatic dishes he had ordered were placed on our table, my stomach betrayed me. It began to growl with hunger. I decided to take in just a small amount of food to silence it. Several minutes later, I had cleaned my plate of appetizers and nodded at the waiter to uncover the steaming lobster dish.

"Delicious, isn't it?" he murmured.

I avoided his eyes which I suspected were smoky blue with amusement. Our silence might have seemed companionable to anyone watching us, I thought, deciding that the old cliche that appearances are often deceptive had never been truer. Who would believe that I had been abducted, forced into a marriage, and was being treated as a captive by this rather good-looking young man? No one. Even now, I couldn't believe it myself!

I could not help but wonder about him. Was he really a lawyer? He had chatted with Professor Lynwood with a polish that might have been developed in a courtroom. But why would such a professional man engage in this kind of deceit and treachery? He must have been collecting information about me for a long time. The thought that he had been a silent observer of all my activities was in itself appalling. One assumed privacy and even now I could not believe how blatantly it had been invaded.

"Did you enjoy following me around and playing the Peeping Tom?" I asked, deliberately baiting him.

"No, as a matter-fact, I found your mundane activities rather boring. You have about as much excitement in your life as a middle-aged matron. I couldn't believe that the only suitor hanging around was that clod, Randell Delany, and it was obvious he was playing up to your father."

"He is not a 'clod' but a very intelligent, ambitious young man. How dare you accuse him of using me to reach my father!"

"No man in love is going to make a threesome with a girl and her father . . . unless he's more interested in the father than the girlfriend."

"That's not true!"

"What isn't true? That you're not his girlfriend . . . or that you made a threesome with your father?"

"Of course, we went places with my father. And why not? We were interested in the same lectures . . . the same university affairs—"

"The same boring faculty teas. No wonder traveling with your Cousin Della offered a little color in your life."

"And you spoiled that!"

"Yes, I'm afraid you won't be traveling anywhere with your cousin—" His eyes took on a flat hardness. He changed the subject.

"I'm glad we are going to have good food for this crossing. The last time—"

"Yes?"

But he had caught himself. He wasn't going to tell me any more. "You make a habit of this . . . crossing the Atlantic under false pretenses?" I prodded.

"I've sailed to Europe before."

"As a bridegroom?"

"No."

"Then you've never been married—?"

"Not until this morning. But now I'm a married man. And you, Charlotte Demorest, are my wife."

The stark truth of that statement was like a malaise suddenly invading my body. The delicious meal sat uneasily on my stomach and I feared that I was going to be sick. My coloring must have changed to a pasty green because he was suddenly solicitous. "I'm sorry . . . I shouldn't have said that. Come on. I'll take you back to our quarters."

Once more he led me through the labyrinth of corridors. My efforts to try and remember the twists and turns were for naught. All the passages looked alike and I had even failed to notice the number on our door the first time. As he paused in front of 123 and took out a key, I filed away the information.

I went immediately to my stateroom and shut the door. I locked the door with a defiant click, hoping that Mr. Adam Demorest would be duly rebuffed by the sound. I was grateful for the private, miniscule water closet. I did not relish having to share one with other travelers. A small hip tub was provided for bathing but I would have to have hot water brought in. A tall wash stand offered a marble basin and cold water from a copper container above it. I splashed my face vigorously and dried it on a sweet-smelling thick towel. My hearty stomach had recovered from its spurt of nausea. Thank God, I wasn't going to be seasick.

I took off the jacket to my traveling dress and hung it up in a built-in wardrobe and then stretched out upon a very comfortable mattress. The bedstead was brass, like those found in the most luxurious hotels and the top azure coverlet richly quilted. The bed linens were white and held the faint scent of a recent ironing. A deeper blue floral wallpaper was flocked and set in square panels between decorative cherrywood moldings. It was difficult for me to believe that I was on a steel ship heading out into the Atlantic.

My steamer trunk still remained pushed against the wall in the midst of my portmanteau and Della's suitcase and hatbox. I closed my eyes against a poignant sense of loss that the sight of my cousin's things engendered. If only she were here now, accompanying me to England as we had planned. How I had looked forward to traveling with her! I wondered about her "accident". I did not intend to be kept in the dark about her whereabouts. Adam

Demorest thought he had chosen the right young woman to carry out some malevolent scheme but I intended to show him how wrong he was. I vowed that I would not be duped into letting down my guard for one minute.

I must have slept then, a deep weariness overwhelming me. I awoke nearly two hours later. Only the sound of hidden engines and water lashing outside the porthole accompanied the soft swish of bedcovers as I threw them back. It was chilly and I wished that the advertised fireplaces had been placed in the bedrooms instead of the sitting room. I would love to light one and sit before it to warm my body and still my loneliness, I thought.

Listening at the door which opened into the sitting room, I couldn't tell if my jailer was there waiting for me to come out. I quietly turned the lock and cracked the door so I could look out. The room was empty. His door was closed.

I eased out of my stateroom and crossed the sitting room with furtive, light steps. I held my breath as I reached the hall door. As if testing the security of my prison, I turned the polished knob, praying that I would find it open. The door was locked. I knew then what I had suspected. I was not free to come and go. I stilled an urge to pound upon it with both fists.

"You must be feeling better Charlotte?"

I swung around. He was casually leaning in the doorway of his stateroom. He had removed his jacket and silk cravat. His white shirt was open at the collar and his raven hair was ruffled as if he might have been napping also. I don't know why his masculine dishabille disturbed me. My anger was fueled by his appearance. It suggested an intimacy that was insulting as well as sounding a warning bell. We were alone and, by all outward appearances, a newly married couple. I realized then that my own hair was mussed from my nap and I nervously tried to smooth it back and catch the trailing strands that had escaped the twisted coil.

"It looks nice that way." He moved toward me in that graceful, feline way of his. Then he reached out and very gently touched the tousled curls. "I'd like to see it loose on your shoulders." His tone was soft and hypnotic. "I bet it looks like a flaming cataract falling against that white skin."

No man had ever said such things to me. His touch made me quiver, not from fear. His touch was not abhorrent as it should have been. Something that had lain dormant within my body was fired by a response to his nearness and his warm, hypnotic eyes that held me in a trance. He was the devil, weaving a spell that I could not fight. For some unbelievable reason, I was mesmerized by his soft voice and gentle touch. It was as if we had just met. I forgot who I was . . . and what he was. I tried up to call up my anger as a protection against him but it deserted me and was replaced by an emotion I could not identify.

His hands loosened the pins in my rebellious

hair and threaded the thick strands through his fingers. "Beautiful," he said huskily. "Too beautiful." Then his hands slid to my shoulders and I knew he was going to kiss me.

"No!" I choked. If I felt his demanding mouth on mine, all would be lost.

"You need to be kissed and fondled . . . and brought to life. You've been wrapped up in a cocoon, waiting to be awakened."

"You promised," I managed to whisper when his lips were poised over mine. I closed my eyes, shutting out the deep black irises of his eyes, now turning a soft, beguiling blue. "You said . . . you promised . . . you wouldn't force me—"

For a moment his hands tightened on my shoulders. Then they dropped away. I opened my eyes. He had moved back. He was still looking at me but his eyes were gray again and his mobile mouth was held in a tight line. He was angry—at me or at himself? I could not tell.

"You must bear part of the responsibility," he said huskily.

"Responsibility—?" I choked.

"For making me forget that I mustn't make love to you." He walked away then, pausing to look back over his shoulder as he reached his door. "We'd better dress for dinner. Professor Lynwood will be expecting us."

6

The first-class dining room occupied the whole width of the ship, had seating for over four hundred people and was decorated with the same opulence as an Italian palace. Beautiful oak flooring and an infinity of Ionic columns stretched before us. They rose proudly to a heavily decorated ceiling set in squares of white and gold molding. Long tables were covered by snowy white linen. Silver and porcelain tableware bearing the Cunard Company's crests graced the tables. Swivel armchairs upholstered in peacock-blue velvet brocade enabled the passengers to sit down comfortably before rotating themselves to face their food. An army of waiters in formal attire sped quickly from one end of the enormous room to the adjoining kitchen where an aromatic cloud wafted from the numerous preparation rooms.

It was rumored that the kitchen staff was in the hundreds and I could believe it as the enormous task of feeding all these passengers overwhelmed me.

I could see that small alcoves around the edge of the room contained small side tables separated by carved screens and mirrors as was today's fashion. I was not surprised that it was to one of these tables that a hotel steward led us when Adam gave him Alexander Lynwood's name. Apparently the professor's prestige was enough to earn him one of the private tables. I was glad that his recent failures and the ridicule he'd received for his disastrous experiments had not completely destroyed his reputation as one of the world's outstanding physicists. At the moment his friendship with my father represented a safe haven and I smiled gratefully at him as he stood to greet us.

His pale blue eyes twinkled as his bushy gray eyebrows rose in appreciation of a cream-colored evening gown which my seamstress had assured me accented my small waist and ivory shoulders. It was the first time I had ever dressed formally for dinner and I felt a little conspicuous until I looked around and saw the elegant silks and satins worn by other women travelers. Most of the ladies had dressed their hair in elaborate coiffures built up with false hairpieces and adorned with jewels and feathers. My thick hair was full enough to rise high in a chestnut pompadour with full natural curls at the back. After the scene with Adam, I had deliberately kept it off my shoulders.

"Good evening, Charlotte . . . and Adam. May I present my niece, Pamela, and my nephew, Larry."

A dark-haired young woman nodded at me with more of a scrutinizing look than a friendly one. She had her uncle's tall stature and a long graceful neck which was accented by a choker of tiny pearls. Large, dark eyes dominated her face; her rather prominent cheekbones and slim nose were in harmony with her aristocratic bearing. I had the impression that she looked down on most people—including me. Only Adam's saturnine handsomeness eased the crispness of her smile and made her eyes flicker with interest. Undoubtedly she was a woman who got what she wanted and I wondered how Adam would handle the situation if Pamela Lynwood's design landed on him.

Her brother, Larry, in contrast, was only of medium height, with light brown hair and a rather square face—but I liked him immediately. His smile was both flattering and friendly as he responded to the introduction. "How nice to meet you, Charlotte. My uncle has been telling us some stories about his Oxford days. He and your father must have been a pair."

As soon as we were seated, Pamela said in rather crisp, British tones, "My uncle tells us you are newlyweds. I would have thought you would have preferred to have a table to your-selves."

I knew then that we had encountered trouble.

This woman was the kind to peel off layers and delight in any secrets she could turn up. Even though I had been hoping to find someone who might see beyond our charade, I suddenly realized how dangerous that might be. If my father's safety rested in my ability to carry out the pretense, I could not allow Pamela Lynwood to turn the matter into some kind of malicious gossip. As steadily as I could, I returned her prying dark-eyed scrutiny. "I was delighted that such an old friend as your uncle was aboard . . . and I wanted to share him with Adam." The first part was true, I thought, and was pleased with the ring of sincerity in my voice.

"And I am delighted to make the acquaintance of such an illustrious family," added Adam smoothly.

Larry laughed. "Not every member of the Lynwood family fits that description, I'm afraid. Only Uncle Alex has been able to carry the banner into high places. My father tried to follow in his footsteps but only managed to lose his share of my grandfather's inheritance with some bad investments."

"Larry," said his sister sharply. "I'm sure these people aren't interested in our family saga." She turned to her uncle. "I hope you don't mind but I invited someone else to join our table. Fredrick Heinlin . . . you remember, he was traveling with Lady Almsbury last year when we went to Ceylon."

"I thought he kind of caught your fancy, Sis,"

teased Larry. "I caught you looking at him in a predatory way."

"Don't be ridiculous!"

"Now, children," admonished the Professor with a wave of his hand. "Spare us your sibling quarrels. Of course it's all right, Pamela, if Mr. Heinlin joins our table. I want this to be a pleasant crossing for everyone. Now, I've ordered champagne to toast the happy bride and groom." He smiled at us in an affectionate, avuncular manner and raised his fluted goblet. "To Charlotte and Adam . . . and many years of happiness."

I can drink to that, I thought, sipping and smiling, even though my interpretation of the toast was different from what Professor Lynwood had intended. He hadn't added the definitive word, "together".

Pamela's friend arrived and I was surprised to find him a boyish, blond youth who must have been at least five years younger than Pamela. I figured she was close to thirty and he was no more than twenty-five. He was tall and slender and I could appreciate his Germanic handsomeness. He shook hands with Adam and then gave me a polite bow. His eyes met mine with a flirtatious glint that he probably used on all women, six to sixty, including a happy new bride. "Delighted." He kissed my hand and his debonair mustache tickled my skin. "Call me Freddy."

He made me feel quite feminine and I knew

that Pamela did not appreciate my reaction. I wanted to laugh and wink back at him. His addition to our table was like the addition of bubbling champagne. Both the Professor and Larry were good conversationalists but they chose subject matter that was rather stilted and ponderous. Freddy immediately made us all laugh with humorous anecdotes collected in his travels. He was a salesman for a German clock company and I didn't doubt that his outgoing personality made him successful at meeting new people and getting orders from them, as well as finding agreeable feminine companions in his travels. He was placed on my left and I put Adam out of my thoughts and concentrated on enjoying him and the Lynwoods.

The food was delicious. Beginning with a wild game pate with a cumberline sauce, the dishes kept coming—baked French onion soup gratinee, a seafood and pasta salad followed by the main entree, veal piccate covered with an egg-cheese batter and sauteed in olive oil. Vegetables lurked under the most delicious sauces and were almost as good as the desserts offered on a huge tray by a fawning waiter at the end of the meal.

I found myself laughing at Freddy's amusing stories and some anecdotes the Professor told about college days with my father. Only when I caught Adam's unreadable gaze upon me did the mirth dry in my throat and my stomach contract. He played the attentive bridegroom very well. "More champagne, darling? . . .

Delicious sauce, isn't it? . . . Sweetheart, would you like something more from the dessert cart?" Several times his gray eyes lowered slightly in a warning if I refused his solicitations too sharply.

I let him handle all the lies about our fabricated courtship. When the Professor posed questions about Adam's professional career or some personal question about his background, I found myself listening as intently as anyone. I couldn't tell if his answers were the same kind of lies as our courtship and marriage or if he really had been raised in Boston, the son of a prominent physician. Had he really gone to Harvard Law School? Did he have a practice in Boston? Afloat on the Atlantic Ocean, there was no way that I could check up on any of the things he said. He knew it and his quiet arrogance infuriated me.

I had not forgotten the soft, caressing way he had loosened my hair, nor the way he had deftly turned the blame upon me. "You must bear part of the responsibility," he had said as if his advances were part of my making. He had been angry about the incident. But not as furious as I was. How dare he touch me at all, let alone force his kisses upon me and stroke my hair in that wanton fashion. Even now in this glittering dining room, I felt heat rising into my face as I remembered the way I had allowed his caresses.

I lowered my eyes, touched the white napkin to my lips, and then looked up to find Freddy

Heinlin's eyes upon me. My flush had not gone
unnoticed and his boyish grin told me he knew
that my thoughts had been filled with an
embarrassing intimacy of some nature.

Adam caught the look and quickly covered my
hand with his. He whispered, "Very good. The
blushing maiden is just exactly right."

I wanted to jerk my hand away and slap his
face. He must have known I was embarrassed
remembering what had happened between us.
What a devious and calculating person he was! I
suspected that he had even deliberately created
the intimacy between us so I would have something to blush about. Everything about him
reeked of satanical intent. I dreaded going back
to the suite with him.

When Larry suggested after dinner that we go
into one of the salons where an orchestra had
been provided for dancing, I readily agreed. It
was only after the six of us had been seated near
a small dance floor that I realized my mistake.

"A wedding waltz," Professor Alexander
demanded, smiling at me as he summoned a
waiter and sent his request to the musician's
platform. "A dance to celebrate the happy
occasion."

"No . . . please," I protested.

"No time for modesty," chided Freddy. "Such
a lovely bride should promenade for all to see."

I looked imploringly at Adam. I couldn't do it.
He had to say something to stop the horrible
torture of playing out the charade with everyone's eyes upon us.

He leaned over and kissed my forehead, whispering stridently, "Don't look so frightened. You're a happy blushing bride." He stood up and gave me a loving smile which did not reach his gray eyes. I knew then that he wasn't any happier with the situation than I was.

With everyone's eyes on us, Adam rose and took my hand. There was nothing for us to do but walk out into the center of the floor as everyone clapped and smiled and toasted the newlyweds. My smile was as stiff as cardboard as the strains of a Strauss waltz filled the elegant room. My rigidity in his arms made the first few steps we took almost clumsy. He fixed a steady eye on me and smiled wryly. "Don't trip me—"

"Don't tempt me." I growled and smiled broadly.

"You'd look foolish sitting on your backside—"

"Maybe you'd be the one on the floor—"

"Wanna bet?" He laughed and then twirled me in a series of fast spins.

In spite of myself I drew strength from his firm hand on my back and the reassuring squeeze of his other hand. His smooth command of the rhythm overcame my stiffness and I responded to his firm lead as we moved to three-quarter time. Dancing came naturally to me. The faculty was always invited to school socials and, of course, I accompanied my father as his partner to all the college dances.

Although most of my evenings were taken up dancing with other faculty members, some of them were very adept dancers and I didn't mind in the least that they were not romantic partners. It was the music, the graceful movement that made it such a pleasure—not the closeness of any partner. Never had I been so painfully aware of a man's arms around me and the slight pressure on my back which pulled me close to his invading warmth. I forgot about the people watching us as our bodies moved together in the harmony of the music and floating steps. The sensation was nothing I had ever experienced before. I did not want to respond to that dark head bent close to mine but a strange tingling enveloped me as his breath touched my face with a now familiar masculine scent.

"You make a beautiful bride," he said, his gaze bathing my face. "I bet every man in the room is wishing he were here in my place."

It was only this morning that he had touched me for the first time, forcing my lips to breathe his name as his demanding kisses softened my mouth, but he had wrought a frightening change in me. He had made my body aware of desire—a forbidden hunger that invaded my limbs despite any rational protest. His lips touched my hairline in a quick kiss as we whirled to the music. It was a swift, light caress and I stiffened against an impulse to lean into him. The music, the awakening of my own femininity, and the danger of such sensual responses combined to create a dizzy excitement.

"Smile," he said softly and I knew then that the tender kiss was a part of the performance. It helped steady my emotions.

"I hate you," I said through smiling teeth.

"I know." Something flickered in his eyes and then was lost. Only his lips remained softly curved. "You did very well at dinner . . . but I don't think you should allow Freddy to become too friendly."

"Why not?"

"Didn't you see the dagger eyes Pamela sent in your direction every time he spoke to you? She's one jealous wildcat—and we don't need that kind of complication. It would be better if you didn't make any conquests during the crossing."

I knew my eyes had widened. "Conquests?"

"Don't pretend that you were unaware of Freddy and Larry acting like schoolboys performing for a pretty girl! It didn't get by Pamela. I thought you were deliberately flirting with them to get back at me. Don't do it! It's much too dangerous—for everybody."

I wanted to laugh in his face. I had been enjoying making some new friends, nothing more. Of course, I responded to their stories but there had been nothing flirtatious in my laughter or romantic interest. He was making it all up to keep me from encouraging their friendship. The only danger for me lay in keeping myself isolated.

He shouldn't have warned me because when we returned to our table, I deliberately set out to cement the friendships which offered an escape from him. I danced repeatedly with both Larry and Freddy and even coaxed Professor Lynwood out on the floor.

I knew I was drinking too much champagne. A little glass of sherry with my father on some special occasion was the limit of my tolerance for spirits. Adam tried to thwart my acceptance of more champagne each time it was offered but I managed to drink considerably more than I would have under normal conditions.

He danced with me several times and the last time, I was so light and dizzy that I stumbled. Without even taking me back to the table, he eased me through the crowd and out the door before I had a chance to protest.

"We . . . we just can't leave like that."

"Of course we can."

"But what will they think?"

His smile was patient. "We're newly married, remember? This is our wedding night. They will understand—"

Wedding night! The words were a harsh clanging in my head. I stumbled.

"You drank too much," he said as he steadied me.

He kept his arm around my waist as we reached the promenade deck. The brisk night breeze touched my face with refreshing coolness. He was right. I was feeling the effect of all that champagne. My legs seemed detached from my body, threatening to fold under me, and my head reeled with a bewildering, fuzzy sensation. I reached out and grabbed the railing, leaning up against it for support.

"I tried to stop you—"

"Don't lecture me," I snapped, keeping my eyes away from his stony profile and staring at the silvery ocean. Ribbons of moonlight spread across the waters, rising and falling, in ever-changing patterns like liquid sculptures. I thought, melodramatically, of throwing myself overboard. Tears welled up in my eyes and I heard myself sobbing.

"Don't—" he put his arm around my shoulders.

I tried to shrug it off but he only held me more tightly. "Take it easy—"

"Why did you have to do this to me?" I sobbed. "Why couldn't you leave me alone? It was going to be a wonderful trip. I couldn't believe it when cousin Della asked me to go . . . I planned it for such a long time—"

"Charlotte . . . I'm sorry. Believe me, I wish there was some other way . . . but there isn't. It's going to be all right . . . please trust me—"

A strangled harsh sound coming from my throat made me cover my face with a fist to choke back the sobs. He had callously destroyed my world as thoroughly as if he had deliberately thrown something breakable against a stone wall. The jagged pieces could never be put back together again. No matter what happened on this voyage, or when we reached land again, I could never put aside the traumatic upheaval he had brought into my life. Even if my father remained unharmed and Cousin Della recovered from her "accident," I would never be the same. He had turned my world into a horrible, fragmented chaos. "I hate you," I sobbed again, unable to find any other words to throw at him.

"You're tired. It will go easier from now on. Come on, let's go below."

"No! I don't want to go with you . . . ever!"

"I see. You're prepared to sleep on deck . . . or in one of the lifeboats?" He sighed, and a deep weariness was evident in his voice. "Yes, I suppose you would . . . if I'd let you. But unfortunately, the bride must sleep with the groom tonight. It wouldn't look right, otherwise . . . and all this elaborate pretense would be for nothing. You've conducted yourself very well, Charlotte. Your father would be proud of you."

He had found my Achilles' heel. How callously he was using it to keep me cooperating. My father—what would he say to all of this? I could hear his bombastic voice in my ears as loudly as if he were standing at the railing with me. "Don't do it, Charlotte! Don't let yourself be manipulated by anyone." He'd never approve of me cooperating with this abductor but I knew that if the positions were reversed, he would do the same for me. I sniffed back my tears, raised my head, and turned around.

"All right. You win, again. I'll play your little game."

"Good." He was obviously relieved that in my inebriated state, I wasn't going to throw some kind of an embarrassing scene.

I let him keep his arm around my shoulders as we made our way down the steps and along the corridor to our room. It was particularly in these narrow passages that I had the feeling of being in the depths of a ship. The rest of the accommodations were like those of a hotel. I hated the closed-in, buried sensation of the long corridors.

He unlocked our door and then turned to me. I had the absurd feeling that he was going to carry me over the threshold. I backed up as if to evade his touch. He frowned. "After you," he said politely with a wave of his hand.

I found that I couldn't move.

"Charlotte—" There was a warning edge to his voice.

I raised my chin and swept past him in a rather wobbly, regal manner.

I could have sworn I heard him snicker. My fuzzy head seemed to be attached to some kind of a swivel. The floor rose and fell with a movement that had nothing to do with the roll of the ocean. No, I couldn't pass out. I had to keep my wits about me. He manipulated me too easily. My emotions reeled out of control even when I was thinking rationally. What a fool I'd been to drink so much. My fuzzy thoughts whirled.

Rising panic set in. I had made myself vulnerable . . . susceptible . . . helpless. In my present state I had no defense against him. He could do as he wished. Our wedding night, he had said. Everyone would understand . . . everyone would expect the marriage to be consummated. Protests rose in my throat but never made it past my lips.

My legs suddenly floated away from me and just as I crumbled, his strong arms caught me. I wanted to protest as he carried me into my stateroom but somehow the words got lost.

Wedding night! No! No!

I floated away in a thickening darkness that shut out his face and the touch of his hands as he began to undress me.

7

I awoke with a bitter taste in my mouth and with my head thumping louder than the twin-screw engine that drove the ship. For a moment I couldn't remember where I was and I watched a slightly swinging lamp as one hypnotized. Then my thoughts cleared and I stiffened as if suddenly encased in ice. My arms were under the covers as if I had been neatly tucked in the night before. I let my hands slip over my body and realized I was wearing only my lace-trimmed chemise and drawers. My corset, hose, and petticoats were gone. A knowledge as shocking as anything I could imagine made me gasp. Why I should have been surprised at this last evidence of his willingness to humiliate and subjugate me, I didn't know. Any other gentleman would have saved me such an embarrassment. But he was not a gentleman.

He was a deceitful rogue of the first order. *He had undressed me!* And what else? What other liberties had been taken?

I sat straight up. My hair flowed smooth and free over my shoulders with all the pins removed. I crossed my arms over my nearly bare breasts in a foolish gesture of modesty. My horrified gaze fixed on the neat pile of petticoats, my lightly boned corset with its lace-trimmed cover and white hose and white kid slippers. My evening dress must have been carefully hung away and the lavaliere from my neck laid neatly on the built-in highboy. The evidence was there and yet I couldn't believe it. He had boldly taken off my dress, petticoat, corset, stockings and shoes and loosened my hair—all without my knowledge. What else had he done? I touched my lips as if some evidence of his kisses still lingered there. Had he stroked my bare skin, caressed my nearly naked body—and had I responded to him? Horror brought heat up into my cheeks.

How could I have let myself get in such a condition? My determination to keep myself alert had been forgotten in some childish effort to displease him. Last night, I had played right into his hands. The last thing I remembered was my watery knees giving out halfway across the sitting room floor. He had caught me and then brought me in here . . . taken off my dress and tucked me in. I had been completely vulnerable. He could have stripped me naked; instead he had left me partially clothed. *He could have taken complete advantage of me as his lawfully wedded wife—but he hadn't!* The truth suddenly struck me. He had kept his promise. He had not forced himself upon me even when I was in no condition to resist. True, his lack of propriety was deplorable but, begrudgingly, I had to admit that I was no worse off for his having put me to bed. Still, my pride and righteous indignation made me want to lash out at him for his presumptuous behavior.

Getting to my feet was a laborious process. I felt awful. Dressing and completing my morning toiletries was also a slow torture. "Oh—!" I groaned at the slightest movement. The champagne which had been so lovely and benign going down my throat now demanded retribution. I pressed my hands against my head trying to contain the throbbing that made my head swell and retract with each movement.

The tall folding washstand with its hidden tank of water allowed me to splash water on my face, brush my teeth, and dampen my curly hair so that I could pull it back into a rather prim knot at the nape of my neck. No fancy coiffure this morning. In the same mood, I chose a simple white highnecked lawn blouse and a fawn-colored walking skirt and matching long-waisted jacket. My reflection in the washstand mirror satisfied me. I hoped my eyes didn't show the malicious anvil pounding away inside my skull. I straightened my shoulders, took a deep breath to try and settle my queasy stomach. I was determined to show him that I was none the worse for having had too much champagne the night before.

I opened my door and forced myself to sail out into the sitting room like a war frigate ready for battle—but my adversary was not there. With a grateful sigh I let myself slump down in the nearest chair. I had just been there a moment or two when a brisk knock at the door reverberated in my head.

I opened the door to a steward who brought in a breakfast tray. "Your husband ordered it," he said in response to my surprised expression.

"Thank you. Please set the tray down over there." I indicated a small gateleg table set between two cane chairs near one of the large portholes.

"He also asked me to give you this." He handed me a folded note.

I looked at him then, directly in the face, and recognition was like the clap of a thunderbolt. "You!"

"Yes, ma'am."

It was the driver of the hackney cab which had taken me to my Cousin Della's house. The thin, emaciated frame, his narrow face, pointed chin and those deep-set dark eyes were unmistakable. I remembered the fright he had given me when I thought he had been my abductor. Now he was posing as something else. "What are you doing here?" I croaked.

"I'm your steward for the crossing," he said with a slight bow.

Even in his spotless white uniform there was

the air of a derelict about him. His shoulders slumped and I knew there was a hidden chaw of tobacco in his cheek. His uneven teeth were yellow. A name tag on his jacket lapel read, Jasper Beale.

"You're one of them!" I gasped. "What happened to the regular steward?"

"He got sick . . . at the last minute." There was a twitch at the corner of his mouth as if he were repressing a satisfied smile. "So I was persuaded to take his place. Is there anything else, ma'am?"

"Get out!"

"I'll be close by if you need me." He gave me another mocking bow, turned away and ambled out. I knew that his slow, relaxed movement was deceptive. I sensed that he could strike as fast as a viper when necessary. I had the impression he had eyes at the back of his head.

I sat down, weak from the shock that this despicable man was here on this ship and assigned to my cabin. How could it be? How could Adam arrange such a substitution? Was there no end to the elaborate deception? He had arranged for my father's colleague to become ill so my father would have to stay in Philadelphia and now I knew he had arranged for the steward who would have served us to be replaced by an accomplice.

Trembling, I poured a cup of tea from a heavy silver-plated pot. I took several sips to settle my queasy stomach before I opened the note.

"I'll meet you on the promenade deck later

this morning. Fresh air and exercise will be good for your hanghover. Your loving husband. P.S. I told you not to drink so much."

I crumpled up the note and threw it across the room. This childish tantrum only made me feel worse. He was laughing at me and I knew it. Once more I blushed thinking about his having undressed me and touched my nearly naked body. Then I tried to forget the embarrassing event, refusing to give it any importance. I vowed to make certain that such a thing didn't happen again.

After I had had some tea and toast, I felt much more like a human being. I peered out the porthole and saw that it was a lovely, sunny day. Sky and water blended together in an iridescent glow that was enchanting. I knew that fresh air would be good for me and a brisk walk around the deck might clear my head. Despite my determination to do exactly the opposite of what the note had requested, I found my gloves and tied a bonnet on my head. There was an excitement about traveling on this luxury ship that even the bizarre circumstances could not completely erase.

I eased open the door and peered both directions down the corridor. It was empty. If Jasper Beale were lurking somewhere close, I did not see him. I headed down the corridor in a direction which I hoped would take me to the proper stairway. A mounting sense of claustrophobia enveloped me and I hurried my steps when I heard someone coming up behind me.

I jerked around, expecting to see Jasper Beale. It was the blowsy-looking woman whose lewd remarks had embarrassed me yesterday. Maudy Haversham. I couldn't believe the bad luck of running into her again.

"My . . . my . . . it's the blushing bride," she said in her raucous voice. "Looking a little peaked this morning, I do declare." Her deep laugh was knowing. "Didn't get much sleep, I reckon—"

"I slept very well," I said stiffly.

"Well what do you think, dearie?" she demanded in a kind of conspirator's whisper.

"About what?"

"Married life! I wouldn't trade it for anything. I was single a good many years before Mr. Haversham came along. An old maid, I was." She bobbed her feathered bonnet. "Nobody thought I'd ever catch hold of a man like Mr. Haversham. A real gent, he is. Traveling all over the world. Taking me with him. And he knows how to make a gal feel special—if you know what I mean." She winked. "He's not handsome but he doesn't need to be when the lights are out."

Again her bawdy laughter echoed in the corridor and brought an embarrassed coloring up into my cheeks.

"Going to take a stroll, are ye? Where's that handsome bridegroom? In one of the smoking parlors, I'll bet," she said, answering her own question. "Have you seen one of those first-class gentlemen bars? La-di-da, fancy, fancy, fancy. They wouldn't be good enough to crease their trousers in a plain old pub. Gracious, no, they've got to have upholstered benches to sit on and solid wood tables to hold their mugs of ale. Lot different than the pub where Mr. Haversham found me slinging around pints for workingmen. Never could understand what brought a man like that in the Red Rooster Inn, but I ain't complaining. Lucky day for me, it was. Look at me now." She smoothed fuzzy puffs of hair which were a confused mixture of light, dark, and gray. "First class. That's the only way to travel. We just got back from the Orient . . . Shanghai . . . Hong Kong. Ever been there?"

"I've never been out of the United States. But my cousin was there last fall. She said that . . . that we might go East on our next trip." The words echoed hollowly in my ears.

"Well, you'll like England. Nice place for a honeymoon. Are you going to stay long?"

"I don't know. It's up to . . . to my husband." Her prying questions made me wonder what would happen when we reached port? Would my part in this horrible charade be over? I firmed my chin and determined then that I would get some answers from him . . . and soon.

Maudy Haversham knew her way through the labyrinth of halls and stairways and I let her lead the way to the promenade deck.

It was a cheerful sun that greeted us. Rows of

chairs lined the inside deck and travelers were sunning themselves as they read or slept or talked with others who were taking brisk strolls around the ship. Maudy settled herself in one of the wooden chairs and I grasped the welcome opportunity to leave her there, murmuring that I felt like some exercise.

"If your handsome bloke comes looking for you, I'll tell him you went thata way," she cackled and waved goodbye as I took off around the deck.

Her nonstop conversation had not improved my headache. Her lewd snickering about marriage only added salt to an open wound. I was *not* married! I hated the way people referred to my "husband" and forced me to mouth the vile word. Her prying questions had made me realize that this horrible pretense might go on . . . and on. I had no way of knowing when my father would be safe. I stopped at the railing and let my gaze wander to the misty horizon which blended sea and heaven together in a indistinct line. From the sun's direction I knew I was looking back at the North American continent. Everything I knew and loved was being left behind and I feared that I might never see it again.

Blinking back a sudden fullness in my eyes, I hunted for an empty chair and eased it back into a half-reclining position. Closing my eyes helped the pulsating beat of my headache. I tried to relax. For nearly a half-hour I dozed in the warmth of the sun until a childish voice piping in my ear startled me.

"Hi . . . whatcha doing?" A freckled face peered into mine with the brashness of a four year old.

"Resting."

"Why?"

"Because I'm tired."

"Why?"

I knew I was on a nonstop track. I reversed gears. "Who are you?"

"Scotty."

"Where are your parents?"

"I don't know."

"They'll be looking for you."

"No they won't! Nanny will!" He corrected me as if I'd said something stupid.

"Maybe you'd better go find her."

He wore short pants, hightop shoes, and a white shirt with a large soft bow tied under his neck. Thick shocks of red hair fell around his face in waves. He shook his small head. "I'm running away."

I suppressed a smile. His serious expression did not invite levity on my part. "I see. And where are you going to run to?"

He shrugged. "Maybe to Africa."

"I think you're on the wrong ship, fellow," said a familiar masculine voice. I looked up startled as Adam grinned down at the boy and ruffled his hair. "We're heading in the wrong direction, I'm afraid."

"I want to go to Africa!" The youngster pouted and stamped his little foot.

116

"Then you'd better talk to the Captain," Adam said solemnly. "Why do you want to go to Africa?"

"I like elephants. And my father won't let me have one!"

We both laughed and exchanged a moment of amusement as our eyes met.

"What's your name?" Adam asked.

Squinting one eye, the little fellow peered up at Adam. "Scotty . . . what's yours?"

What a handful this wiry, obstinate little boy was, I thought. I didn't envy his parents—or his nanny.

"Adam . . . and I'm afraid you'll have to settle for England instead of Africa."

"No, I'm going to Africa . . . after I go to England. Oh . . . oh . . . here comes Nanny!" Scotty took off in the opposite direction and disappeared around the bow of the ship. A young woman in a gray dress, her cape flapping like wings, ran after him like a goose-girl trying to recapture a flyaway gander.

It was the first time I had heard Adam's deep laughter. It was full and resonant. Tiny laugh lines around his eyes softened his usual austere expression. He looked relaxed with a soft silk scarf blowing around his neck and a dark blue boating jacket accompanying white trousers. For an instant, the net of intrigue that surrounded us disappeared. If only the nightmare would disappear and allow us to follow the magnetic attraction that flowed between us. Even now, my foolish thoughts centered upon him in a way that made me look away quickly as if he might read my mind.

"Cute kid. I'm betting that someday he gets his elephant. He won't let his dreams get away." His dark brows matted for a moment and then he pulled another deck chair close to mine.

"How are you feeling?"

The encounter with the little boy had set a pleasant mood which I was reluctant to break. I found it impossible to take offense at the polite inquiry. "My headache is gone," I answered honestly. "You were right, I drank too much. It won't happen again."

"Spoken in the true form of the 'morning after'," he teased. "You went out like a light last night."

I knew that warmth was creeping up my neck. "I wish you had not taken the liberty of . . . of undressing me!"

"How do you know I did? Maybe I called a maid."

My eyes must have widened with surprise. I had not considered that possiblity. "Did you?"

"No. I had that pleasure myself."

"You . . . you are contemptible! A gentleman wouldn't taken advantage of the situation like that!"

"Oh, I don't know. Some gentleman I know would *not* have settled for a good night kiss."

"You kissed me?"

"It was the least I could do when you looked so angelic with your hair spread out on the pillow and your lips so soft and inviting." His gaze slid to my mouth in a tantalizing deliberateness.

I caught my lower lip in an embarrassed gesture as if the warmth of the secret kiss was still hidden there. "You should have called a maid!"

"I didn't think it would look right . . . our wedding night and all." He smiled slightly, mocking my indignation.

"You . . . you are a despicable cad."

"Please, Mrs. Demorest, people will think we're having our first fight."

"I met Jasper Beale this morning! Your man Friday. Knave of all trades!"

"Yes . . . a very enterprising fellow."

"You arranged for him to replace the regular steward."

"Yes."

"I don't suppose it would do any good to ask you why."

"No, it wouldn't."

He gave me a maddening slow grin that unleashed my ready temper. I swung my legs off the chair and was trying to get to my feet with as much poise as I could. As luck would have it, I turned to find Mr. and Mrs. Haversham barreling down upon us.

"There you are!" gushed Maudy. "Well, well, both gents showed up, didn't they? Just in time for lunch. I was telling Mr. Haversham that you looked a little lost and peaked this morning—" She cackled knowingly.

"Nice to see you folks again." George Haversham's pudgy face was creased with a smile. "Maudy said you might join us for lunch."

"I'm sorry, we're meeting some people in the lounge—" Adam said too readily to be polite as he took my arm.

"That's too bad. Maudy was telling me, Mrs. Demorest, that you have a cousin who travels quite a bit. I was wondering if we might have run into her—"

I felt Adam's hand stiffen on my arm. I glanced at his leathery face and then back at Mr. Haversham's inquiring expression. Suddenly every nerve in my body was vibrating with expectation. Could it be? Could this be the unexpected complication for which I had hoped.

"My cousin's name is Della—," I answered with dry lips.

"McPherson?" he finished triumphantly. Then slapped his fat hands together. "Della McPherson. She was in Hong Kong the same time as we were. Remember, Maudy, the bouncy, dark-haired woman who wore such bright clothes. We kept running into her. And you're her cousin. What do you know? Della McPherson . . . said she was a widow . . . that her husband had been an army man. So she's your cousin. Well, well. Small world, isn't it? Seems to me I remember her saying something about going to London this spring—" His expression was quizzical.

There was a warning squeeze on my arm. I could feel Adam's tension flowing through it.

"I . . . I guess she changed her plans," I said lamely. Now that the moment was here I didn't know what to do with it. I didn't like the Havershams. Appealing to them for any kind of help was repugnant.

"She saw you off, I suspect," grinned Maudy. "Too bad we couldn't have seen her. We love to keep track of all our traveling companions, don't we, George?"

"Yes, indeed. Well now we really must get together—"

"Some other time, perhaps," said Adam smoothly. He smiled down at me as he quickly led me away and I knew from the cold gray in his eyes that he was less than pleased about this new development. "Damn," he muttered.

I should have been pleased by his consternation. Someone on this ship knew my Cousin Della! It was a coincidence which upset him. For some strange reason I felt a nervous tightening in my stomach that wasn't altogether one of joy. If I alerted these people to my aunt's disappearance, what would happen? Would they help me or would they turn out to be a boomerang that I could ill afford if I wanted to keep my father safe?

"I thought we were going to meet someone," I said when I came out of my reverie and found that we were in that stark corridor outside our rooms.

He opened the door without answering and rather abruptly ushered me into it. "I have to think. Perhaps it's best that we play the devoted honeymooners and stay in our quarters as much as possible."

"I won't be shut up like—like a prisoner." My temper instantly flared.

"You're not a prisoner," he countered. "You're a willing hostage."

"Willing!" I gave a scathing laugh. "I don't care for your definition of 'willing'."

"You are cooperating—"

"Only because you have threatened my father with harm if I don't. That's emotional blackmail! And you're not going to get away with it, you know," I taunted, suddenly enjoying this crack in his smooth, calm exterior. The Havershams worried him. It was like a trump card in my hand—if I only knew how to use it. "You can't keep me locked up here, you know. I have friends on this ship. We're expected to eat at the Professors table every evening."

He sat down and he put his head back on the curved cushion of the settee. With his legs stretched out he looked perfectly relaxed and at ease, but I knew differently. He was like an animal that remains absolutely quiet, with every muscle and sinew tensed to spring.

"You're afraid I'm going to tell them about my cousin's so-called accident!" I flounced down in a nearby chair, gloating. This was the first time I had felt that he was vulnerable. He had been manipulating me like a marionette on a string. Now one of those strings had unexpectedly broken. I didn't know how or why . . . but I intended to find out and make use of it to my own advantage. "Cousin Della traveled all over with her husband . . . and after he died by herself. There might be other people on the Lucania who know her." Like a bullfighter placing his sharp barbs, I attacked him. "You thought that you could isolate me while you did your dirty work—whatever that is! Now you know that if something happens to me—"

"Nothing's going to happen to you," he said patiently, "unless you do something very dangerous, like encouraging the Havershams' friendship."

Nothing appealed to me less than that but I wasn't going to let him know it. "Maudy's a gossip," I taunted. "If she senses anything out of the ordinary, she'll never let it rest. Apparently Mr. Haversham found her in some English pub—"

"What kind of business is he in?" The question was swift. He had his head back, his eyes closed as if digesting everything I was saying.

"I . . . I don't know. I don't think she said. Maybe he's just well off. There are people like Cousin Della who spend most of their time traveling. You should have expected that someone would have—"

He looked at me then and the fury in his eyes stopped my breath in my throat. "I don't believe in coincidence." It was a cold, deadly statement as sharp as the blade of a knife.

I flinched as his glare raked my face.

"It isn't an accident that the Havershams are aboard this ship! And you're not going to have any contact with them—do you hear me? You think that this is a chance to alert someone about your cousin, but it isn't! It's a chance to get your lovely head bashed in!"

He pulled me to my feet and lifted my chin with his firm hand, staring directly into my face. "Are you listening to me, Charl? You're going to avoid the Havershams." There was no feathering of blue in his eyes. They were wintry gray with a fiery narrowing that left no doubt in my mind that he would do anything he had to to enforce his statement—even keep me locked up for the rest of the trip. "Do you understand?"

The firm grip he had on my chin would not let me nod so I croaked, "Yes." He looked angry enough to strike me if I refused.

"You won't try to contact them?" His fingers tightened on my chin.

"No."

"Or allow yourself to be alone with them at any time?"

"No."

"Good. I believe you because I don't think you're willing to gamble that you can get away with disobeying me."

He dropped his hand but he did not move away from me. His voice softened. "I don't want to frighten you—"

A hysterical giggle reached my trembling lips. My flesh hurt from the pressure of his fingers on my chin. I knew I was trembling with a mixture of fear and anger.

"I won't hurt you . . . and I'm going to see to it

that no one else puts you in jeopardy. This is serious business. Every move you take could be dangerous. You'll stay in your stateroom unless I'm with you. We'll have dinner with the Professor every night and perhaps attend some of the soirees . . . but stay away from the Havershams!''

I didn't understand why the Havershams posed a threat and the Professor and his family didn't. My pretend husband had not reacted negatively to them at all. I had to ask the question. ''Why is it all right for me to associate with Professor Lynwood . . . and not with the Havershams?''

''Because he doesn't know your Cousin Della.''

8

The next few days aboard ship passed without incident. Whenever I left our staterooms Adam was with me. We certainly gave the impression of being inseparable newlyweds. We walked the decks, explored the ship's library and spent afternoons sitting in the sun, resting or reading. Much to my surprise, sometimes we just talked.

He did not seem interested in card games, shuffleboard or other shipboard activities. "What do you like to do for fun?" I asked.

"When I'm not marrying beautiful young ladies?" he replied with a teasing glint in his eyes. "Well, that doesn't leave me much time . . . but I suppose I do have one weakness."

My ears perked up. "What is that?"

"Horses." He laughed. "Don't look so disappointed. Did you think I was going to confess to some infamous addiction?"

"Perhaps," I admitted. "And I am surprised by your answer."

"Why? I love to ride. There's no excitement like being astride a spirited thoroughbred tossing his head and dancing on four feet. Feeling the wind whipping your face as you give him his head . . . no, there's nothing like it." His eyes sparkled and for a moment a boyish enthusiasm softened the smooth, taut lines of his face. Adam Demorest was not one for superficial emotions. What he felt—he felt deeply. This knowledge was disconcerting. I feared that once he began a course of action, he would not swerve from it.

"I wouldn't think you'd have much chance for riding in Boston."

"I haven't lived all my life in Boston." Then he changed the subject. We appeared to be harmonious and relaxed, the undercurrent of tension between us hidden. Only when the Havershams exchanged greetings with us did Adam's uneasiness transmit itself to me. I did not like to see the cleft deepen between his eyebrows when he was lost in thought. I felt as if some undefined pressure was building and it was all the more terrifying because I didn't know what direction it would take.

Every evening we joined the Lynwood party for dinner. I thoroughly enjoyed the companionable exchanges and the intellectual stimulation. Professor Lynwood was a delightful conversationalist and he entertained us with anecdotes about his twelve-year stay in the United States. I was sorry that his visit had ended on such a sour note. If the experiments he had been conducting for the government had been successful, I doubted that he would be going back to England.

His nephew, Larry, told me in a quiet aside that he had been treated badly by his American colleagues. Instead of being celebrated as a hero for his aerodynamic experiments, he had been ridiculed. I felt embarrassed for my countrymen and I was glad that I had the chance to show him how much my father and I respected him.

I felt sorry for Larry. He confessed he took after his father who had also missed out when the brains and looks were handed out. "Uncle Alex is the only one who has done something with his life. My father wasted his . . . died penniless . . . leaving Pamela and me dependent upon the bounty of Uncle Alex. And I'm as much a failure as my father."

"That's not true," I protested.

"Yes, it is. I wouldn't even be able to keep Uncle Alex's estate running smoothly without Pamela's help. She's got the business head . . . not me."

Occasionally Pamela and Freddy asked us to join them in a foursome. I thoroughly enjoyed Freddy's light flirtatious banter because it chased away my dark and confusing thoughts. This gregarious salesman knew how to infuse any party with a gaiety that made the world seem light and airy. No one was a stranger to

him and every female within the range of his
smile preened and simpered when he gave them
his attention. Pamela seemed to suffer his
gregarious manner the way a mother indulged
an attractive offspring. There was no doubt that
she was utterly and completely smitten by him.
Once I overheard a rather heated conversation
between Freddie and Larry as I came upon
them unexpectedly one day on the promenade
deck. Larry's round face was quite red and he
said something in a choked voice about his
sister's good name. It was obvious that he was
worried about Freddy's way with the ladies. He
was playing the good brother and trying to
protect Pamela. From what I had seen, she was
perfectly capable of taking care of herself . . .
and Freddy. I was certain that Pamela wanted
us to join them for several of the after-dinner
socials and dances because I was married and
not available for any serious flirtation. In my
case, I was glad Adam accepted the invitations.
It was easier to be in the company of other
people than alone with him.

I watched my intake of champagne and wine
for I was determined to keep my wits sharp and
try to determine why Adam Demorest was
uneasy every time the Havershams came near
me. Several times, I found George Haversham's
gaze fixed on me and I wondered what I would
do if he asked me to dance or if he and Maudy
tried to join our table. Neither thing happened
and I began to think that my pretend husband
was unduly alarmed that they would try to use

the fact that they had met my Cousin Della to force their company upon us.

One afternoon, I had just finished dressing for a musicale to be held that afternoon in the music room when I remembered the hatbox and suitcase that belonged to Cousin Della. Impulsively, I drew them out from under the bed where I had pushed them out of sight and forgotten them until then.

She must have packed them and set them in the hall before meeting with her "accident", I reasoned. For some reason my hands trembled slightly as I removed the lid of the striped hat box and lifted out a pretty pink hat with silk flowers and a white ostrich feather adorning a wide brim. It was just the kind of lavish hat which my cousin adored and tears filled my eyes with a poignant sense of loss. It was brand-new and she must have bought the hat to wear on our trip. Just looking at her hat was a painful reminder of her absence.

My fingers trembled as I loosened the straps on an alligator suitcase that she must have purchased on one of her travels. The scent of her perfume filled my nostrils as the lid went back, revealing carefully folded garments, a small jewelry box, several bottles of toiletries and one pair of shoes. It seemed to be an overnight bag as if she had wanted to be prepared in case her steamer trunk failed to arrive. For the first time, I wondered where her trunk was. Had it been taken off when the arrangements were changed? I determined to ask Adam—

although any hope of a direct answer was pure foolishness on my part.

I opened the black lacquer jewelry box which had an Oriental design on the lid. It contained several strings of beads, mostly glass or carved bone, and some colorful bracelets and brooches. No pearls or diamonds, just the kind of costume jewelry which my cousin liked. I sat back on my heels and took everything else out and laid it on the floor beside me. There was nothing unusual in the suitcase. The bottles of toiletries contained a pink hand lotion made of glycerin and rose water, a green bottle was a scented bath oil, and several jars of face cream were familiar to me because I had seen similar ones on her dressing table. Combs and hairpins rattled in a tin box.

There was nothing out of the ordinary in the suitcase. Nothing. I unfolded all the clothes, looking carefully at her lacy undergarments and a beautiful piece of cream silk with borders of embroidered gold, the kind Cousin Della liked to drape around her like a Hindu sari. There was a lovely Oriental fan made of embroidered silk and several linen handkerchiefs. Disappointment assailed me. I didn't know what I had expected to find. Perhaps another note or letter or communication that would clarify the reason Adam Demorest did not want me to contact anyone who had known Cousin Della.

I jumped as Adam knocked on the door. "Are you ready—?"

"Yes . . . no—"

He opened the door and caught me sitting there in the middle of the floor surrounded by the things I had just taken out of the suitcase. I tried to mask any expression of guilt.

I must have succeeded for his tone was teasing as he asked, "Hunting for something? I thought you'd unpacked all your things."

He didn't know the suitcase was Aunt Della's! He must have thought her things had been left at the house. "Yes . . . I wanted to . . . to carry this fan. I had to take everything out to find it." I gave a false laugh as I stuffed everything away . . . in a disarray that would have infuriated my cousin. For some reason I didn't want Adam to know that I had her things. He might take them away and I would never have the chance to examine them again.

He reached down and offered a hand to help me up. I would have liked to refuse for I avoided any physical contact with him but I didn't want to give him a chance for any second thoughts about the suitcase. He was looking a little puzzled and I knew in another minute his sharp mind would have found something incongruous in the situation.

"Thank you," I said as I bounded up lightly with his help. "I guess I'm ready. What do you think? Is this the right afternoon dress for a musical soiree?" I wanted to direct his attention away from Cousin Della's things.

One black eyebrow rose. "You're asking for my approval?"

133

"Yes."

"And if I don't give it?"

"I'll wear it anyway."

"Then I guess it's a good thing that I heartily approve." His gaze traveled over the moss green organdy with its puffed sleeves, tight bodice and skirts layered in lace-trimmed flounces. I knew the color was flattering to my hair and the greenish tint in my eyes. He complimented me on my choice. "The fan does add the right touch . . . but I hope you aren't going to turn into one of those simpering females who giggle and hide behind it like a French coquette."

I had to laugh. "A French coquette? It might be fun." I fluttered the fan and blinked my eyes.

"It wouldn't suit you."

My feminine vanity was wounded. "Why not?"

"You're much too—" He hunted for a word.

"Uninteresting?" I offered, bristling.

"Unsophisticated." He smiled broadly and I was startled by the change it made in his face. "You don't need any feminine fripperies. You're very attractive just as you are." Before I could react, he bent his head and kissed me very tenderly on the lips.

I must have closed my eyes for when I opened them, he had stepped back. "That was just to prove my point. Now come on, let's go listen to some fat soprano abuse our ears."

The soprano wasn't fat and she had a beautiful voice. A dark-haired, stately woman sang selections from Madame Butterfly and the poignant laments and loneliness of a woman deserted by her lover touched a chord within me. I knew that basically I was an utter romantic. I had wanted to find my Prince Charming and live happily ever after. My dreams had always included a touch of a Cinderella fairy tale. Perhaps that was the hardest part of this detestable charade. Something deep within me longed to be on a real honeymoon and not married to someone who had chosen me because I fit some nefarious qualifications. I would never forgive him for destroying my dreams. As the music poured over me, tears were close and I must have trembled for he reached over and took my gloved hand.

I bit my lower lip and composed myself, refusing to look at him.

Afterwards, he commented on my reaction to the selections. "You really got carried away, didn't you? It's only a story set to music."

"It's true, nevertheless. And that's what makes it so poignant. Don't you understand? She was a woman who fell in love with an American who never came back to her. She gave him everything and he abandoned her. That's the way men are—"

"Not all men," he countered. "There are happy endings. If a man truly loves a woman—"

"Yes?'

"He'd swim all the way to China to be with her." The smile he gave me made my foolish heart flip over.

That was two times in one day he had come

out from behind his armor and revealed himself to me. I knew that I should use this softening in his behavior to my advantage. If I could detach myself and use his attention I might be more sophisticated than he thought! If I could get past his barbed barriers, I might know how to free myself and protect my father as well.

I deliberately slipped my arm through his as we made our way to a first-class salon for tea. Impulsively, I fluttered my fan and peered over the edge at him. We both laughed and I suddenly found I was not pretending. I liked the warm feeling between us. This knowledge was enough to make me stop such flirtatious foolishness.

Larry joined us and I was grateful for the presence of a third person. I had seen him dancing with several single women at the evening socials and once or twice he had been playing shuffleboard with a group but most of the time he was a loner. "I've decided to dress up as Julius Caesar for the costume ball," he said, his round face creasing in a broad smile. "I figure I might as well be an emperor while I have the chance. What about you, Charlotte? Will you be my Cleopatra?" He looked wistful and I was embarrassed to realize he was serious.

I looked at Adam questioningly. "Are we going?"

"If you want to, darling."

The endearment took me by surprise. He usually called me "Charl" which seemed intimate enough for our charade.

"But, of course, she wants to," laughed Larry. "Women love these things. The costume ball is the most popular affair of every crossing."

"What about costumes?"

"Oh, they're provided, all kinds, for an exorbitant fee, of course. I suspect that the Cunard company buys up costumes from down-and-out theatrical groups. Anyway, it's loads of fun."

I couldn't help but catch some of his enthusiasm. That night at dinner everyone was talking about the masquerade ball. Freddy and Pamela had decided to come as Romeo and Juliet and their shipboard romance seemed to be developing nicely. Professor Lynwood was pleased that he had found something to wear. The fact that Adam was less than excited about the affair only fueled my own interest in the party. I even suggested there might be a theatrical costume that would suit his personality and offered to help him pick it out.

"Thank you, but I doubt that I would feel comfortable in horns and a forked tail."

I laughed and realized that I had been thinking of him more as a seventeenth century nobleman with a feathered hat, rich doublet, breeches and embroidered hose. In fact, I suddenly decided he looked like Van Dyke's portrait of James Stewart. The color of the hair was wrong but the tall, slender, imperious carriage was a good match. His unruffled demeanor was definitely haughty enough to be royal.

"All right. What's making your eyes twinkle in amusement?" he pried.

"I was just picturing your legs in tights."

"If that's a challenge, I must pass."

"Coward!"

"If wearing absurd skintight pants is a test of courage, I confess to a deep-seated yellow streak."

"I'm glad you admit to some imperfection. I didn't know that you were ashamed of your physique," I taunted. "Freddy is willing to show his legs off."

"And so am I—in private. If you are interested—?"

"No!" I said shortly and shut out the sound of his deep laughter.

I decided to make use of my cousin's embroidered sari and I wondered if she had packed it especially for the masquerade dance. It was like her to be prepared for such a social affair. She had promised me a trip I wouldn't forget. How ironic that her promise had come true—without her.

Caught up in the excitement of the masquerade ball, I put aside hovering shadows like a young child putting a blanket over her head, foolishly thinking she's invisible and protected.

Everything promised a gala affair. Elaborate decorations turned the largest salon into a glittering palace; a stupendous feast kept chefs in the kitchen round the clock; an orchestra and entertainment had been secured to present an evening of heightened pleasure. Everything cooperated—except the weather. All day long a storm gathered. Huge swells of water made the ocean choppy and caused the ship to list as it rolled with the undulating current. Even the glow of electric lights could not keep the gray gloom at bay. Lowering clouds and intermittent rain had kept everyone from the promenade decks. Some unfortunate souls with weak stomachs took to their berths and gave up all hope of joining the festivities.

I was glad to spend most of the afternoon in my stateroom. Adam disapeared and Jasper Beale let me know that he was positioned outside my door if I needed anything. I had stopped resenting his presence. He or Adam were always close by wherever I went and some undefined uneasiness made me grateful for it. I had become as fearful as Adam that something would happen to destroy our charade and put my father in danger. More than ever, I believed that Adam was under some authority who could act independently if something went wrong.

He was waiting for me when I came into the sitting room that evening and stood up at my entrance. I was foolishly disappointed to see him conservatively dressed in a U.S. Navy captain's uniform. Although the white suit and brass buttons were a handsome contrast to his dark hair and tanned complexion, I would have preferred to see him in the kind of outfit Freddy

Heinlin and Larry would be wearing. I should have known he wouldn't let a frivolous party break through his stiff decorum. Then I decided that a captain's uniform suited him. He gave orders with the same kind of autocratic, no-nonsense authority.

"You don't approve," he said, reading my tart evaluation.

"I was just thinking you had chosen something that fits your personality, after all.'

"And I might say the same for you. I had been anticipating Marie Antoinette or Madame Pompadour. Instead, you have chosen an Indian sari that covers you from head to toe."

I bristled against his criticism. "Sorry to disappoint you."

"Oh, I'm not disappointed. I compliment you on a very good choice. There is more fascination in feminine mystery than in a flagrant display of a woman's charms."

"I didn't choose it with the intent of fascinating anyone!"

"I know . . . and that makes it all the more enticing." His soft tone made me blush. He was the most maddening, infuriating man I had ever met. I never knew whether he was complimenting or ridiculing me. And I was angrier with myself for even caring!

At the door of the huge salon, we were given half-masks to cover our eyes and for a moment I thought they would change us all into strangers but in the milling crowd, I readily identified Professor Lynwood in his safari hunter's

140

costume with hard helmet and rifle. Pamela made a rather severe Juliet in a midnight-blue gown and her long neck encased in pearl chokers. As Romeo, Freddy's blond handsomeness was enhanced by his velvet doublet and small, soft hat. He smiled appreciatively at the soft oyster-white silk draped over my long, chestnut hair and gallantly kissed my hand as a true Romeo. I felt Adam stiffen at my side and took a perverse pleasure in complimenting Freddy in glowing terms over his choice of costume.

Larry made a perfect Julius Caesar with his rather square, thick build and the wreath of olive leaves around his head made his forehead seem even broader. "Friends, Romans, Countrymen, lend me your ears." His brown eyes twinkled behind his half-mask and he launched into a short memorized speech from Shakespeare's *Julius Caesar*. We all laughed and clapped when he had finished.

As always the food was superb: chicken Montane, sauteed with lemon butter, capers, and topped with shrimp; roast duckling in orange sauce; numerous specialty dishes which I could not fully identify but which complemented the main entrees and made a colorful display of culinary art.

Music hovered as a counterpoint above the dinner conversation and laughter. I looked about and recognized Maudy Haversham in a wild gypsy costume but I did not see her husband sitting at the long table with her. I wondered if he had been one of the unfortunate travelers taken with seasickness. The ship was still pitching as it plowed through the rough waters but the motion only added to the excitement of the evening. Outside the wind and rain pounded on the portholes like disgruntled guests left outside. Suddenly, it was rather frightening to realize that this glittering room was just a speck of light on a black, angry ocean. An eerie sensation of complete helplessness overtook me.

"What's the matter?" Adam touched my arm. "Aren't you having a good time?"

"I was just listening to the storm . . . and I suddenly realized that this floating palace could be swallowed up in it."

"The Lucania is a very safe ship. I'm sure she's capable of weathering worse storms than this—"

"But she's new and she hasn't been put to many tests, has she? What if . . . what if she has a weak spot somewhere? I was realizing how helpless we are . . . and how big the ocean is—"

"Don't think about it. Shall we dance? They're playing *our* waltz—"

The possessive pronoun startled me. Through the slits in his white mask his eyes were dark but a soft glint matched the curve of his lips. My heart did a foolish flip-flop into my throat. I knew I should have given a curt refusal. Giving in to an impulse to be in his arms was pure stupidity and I knew it. But suddenly I wanted to feel the protection of those strong arms.

ILLUSIONS

I rose and let him guide me out onto the dance floor. His arms went firmly around my waist and he drew me close. As we began to move to the romantic strains of the Strauss waltz, I could not break the eye contact between us. Suddenly there was no one in the room except the two of us. The storm, the music, the chatter and laughter all faded away. If love casts a spell as all the poets claim, I felt it descend upon me. I knew then that despite all the unanswered questions, I had become a willing hostage. As we whirled the length of the room, the silk sari slipped off my head but I did not care. I let my long hair swing freely in the air and acknowledged a warmth of desire rising in me as our bodies flowed together in an effortless rhythm. I knew we made a striking couple; my chestnut hair flowing free and his dark wavy head bent close to mine.

When the music ended, we did not draw apart but stood close together, looking at each other and waiting for the music to begin again. I don't know how many times we danced together; but the rest of the world was lost to me. My senses were filled with a bewildering need to be in his arms, feel his fingers gently splayed against my back and his dark head bent so close to mine that his masculinity was like a heavy perfume drugging me. My mesmerized state might have lasted until the last note of music floated away if we had not been roughly pulled out of our romantic reverie.

Because Adam was in a Captain's uniform, a

distraught young woman grabbed his arm as we were just about to resume dancing. "Captain! You must do something! Please . . . please—"

"I'm not the Captain. What is it?" Adam jerked off his mask.

"My little boy, Scotty. He's run away from his nanny. He's out there! In the storm! Oh dear God, what'll I do?"

"Are you sure? Maybe he's just hiding somewhere—"

"No, she saw him go out! But she was afraid to follow him. The wind . . . and lashing waves . . . she came to find us. Oh my God, what are we going to do?"

"Find the Captain! And I'll see if I can find him." He turned to me. "You stay here."

"No, I'll help too," I protested.

"Stay here!" He left me at our table and pushed his way out past the merrymakers. I didn't want him to go out in that storm. Just listening to it terrified me. An overwhelming sense of urgency sent me after him. "Adam! Wait. Let the crew hunt for him."

Either he didn't hear me or chose not to listen. In the next instant he was out of my sight as he jerked open an outside door to the promenade deck and disappeared into the raging darkness outside.

I started to follow when a firm hand stopped me. "You go below. . . . Wait in the stateroom."

I recognized Jasper Beale's beak-like nose and pointed chin even though he was dressed in a clown's costume and wore a half-mask. There was nothing merry about the way he propelled me down the steps.

"No. Go help him," I protested, my voice rising with sudden panic. "He could be swept overboard."

"I'll take you below first."

"No! Please . . . let me go. He needs us—both of us!"

"You wait below." Despite my protests, his claw-like, guiding hand led me down the steps to the lower corridor. There, the muffling of the storm in this silent hall was even more terrifying than the sound and fury of wind and rain. If the walls of the ship gave way and the water came rushing in . . . As this scenario took shape in my mind, I was so frightened of it that at first I didn't realize what was happening.

From out of nowhere, a black hooded figure suddenly came up behind us.

I screamed. A black arm raised and Jasper slumped to the floor, struck from behind. Blood spurted down his face. A wrench fell to the floor beside him.

Screaming, I backed up, trying to evade the black-hooded monk as he lunged at me. He would have had me in his grasp if Jasper hadn't somehow sat up, grabbed his leg, and put the attacker off balance. "Run . . . run," he croaked as he held on to the leg, giving me a chance to get away.

I sped back the way we had come with the black creature after me.

"Help . . . Help!" I screamed, praying that

someone would come to my aid. All the stateroom doors remained shut.

Gasping for breath, and tripping in my long skirt, I bounded up the first staircase, knowing I was lost in the depths of the ship. All my feeble sense of direction was gone. As if in an endless nightmare, I ran through a maze of corridors, first this way and then that. With the creature right behind me, I bounded up another set of stairs and finally reached an outside door. With a strength born of terror, I jerked it open. In the next instant I was outside in the storm.

Water sprayed over the promenade deck like a crazed waterfall. The lashing waves took away my breath and nearly pulled me off my feet. Frantically I grabbed a brass railing on the inside wall and held on to the slippery metal as the floor of the promenade deck became a rising flood. If my pursuer came after me, I knew I would have to forgo the brass railing and run, taking my chances on the slippery promenade deck. I peered through the darkness. The door to the deck remained closed. My pursuer had chosen not to follow me out into the fury of the storm.

I wondered how long I could stay there, pressed up against a wall, and clinging to the brass railing as waves washed over me, tugging at my drenched hair and thin sari. My wet hair whipped across my face as the wind drove my breath back down my throat.

Then I heard it—a childish cry at odds with the winds boisterous wailing. My head came up, and I frantically brushed hair out of my eyes. My faulty sense of direction had been compounded by my frantic flight but I knew that I had come out a different door from the one through which Adam had disappeared.

"Scotty! Scotty!"

I listened with all the acuity my ears would give me. I heard nothing. It had been my imagination.

No, there it was again! Somewhere farther down the deck. Holding on to the railing as if it were a lifeline, I eased my way through the deluge of water and wind. I knew that if I let go, I was in danger of being swept out with the next white-foamed wave.

"Scotty! Where are you?"

This time the high-pitched cry was closer.

I peered ahead over the vacant deck. All of the lounge chairs had been taken in. In the wash of pale light, I couldn't see anything that looked like a small boy huddling on the deck.

I heard the cry again. I held my head in that direction. It seemed to be coming from somewhere over the water. That couldn't be. No little boy could survive more than a couple of minutes in that fury. Scotty couldn't be out there. It was my imagination. I wanted to cover my face and let disappointment give way to tears.

All strength went out of my body. The vicious attack upon Jasper, the threat to my own safety, worry about Adam somewhere in this treacherous storm combined to defeat me.

"Adam . . . Adam—" I sobbed. I was too tired to make my way back inside. It was a movement and not a sound that finally provided a new spurt of energy. I brushed away the dripping strands of hair and squinted into the darkness. At first my brain wouldn't register what my eyes were seeing. I blinked and rubbed my eyes. Yes. It was there! I was not hallucinating. A tiny head was silhouetted against the silver stream of rain and diffused light. It seemed to be suspended in midair. Then I gave a shriek of recognition.

Scotty! The lifeboats! He was in one of them. The boats were held in a high frame out over the water.

"Scotty!" I screamed.

He stood up.

"No . . . no! Stay there—"

I don't think he understood me. He heard the voice . . . but not the words. I saw with horror that he was going to try and climb down.

"No, Scotty, no!" I screamed into the wind and rain. If he left the protection of the lifeboat, he would be swept off that high perch. He must have climbed up there before the storm had reached its present velocity. "Stay there . . . stay there—"

I had to go back for help. But was there time? No, the little boy was moving. I opened my mouth to yell at him again when out of the corner of my eye, I saw a dark, hunched figure braced against the wind coming toward me.

The black monk! He had come after me! I let

go of the railing. Almost instantly a wave caught me. It lifted me off my feet with treacherous gentleness and tugged me toward the outside railing. In the next instant I was pulled away from the swirling black cauldron that had beckoned to me.

"My God! What in hell are you doing out here?" swore Adam, his face glistening with rain and his black hair plastered down on his head. He held me against a pillar, holding on to keep us from being swept overboard and trying to protect my body from the rising and falling waves.

"Scotty . . . he's up there!" I pointed to the suspected lifeboat and saw with horror that the little boy had not heeded my words. He was trying to climb down the high frame holding the boat above the water.

"Hold on—and don't move!"

In the next instant Adam was at the railing. Horror froze in my chest. He was going to try and climb up the slippery metal frame. The girder was constantly being washed by water, almost obliterated from view by white foam. *Don't do it!* The words never left my throat as I saw his dark frame battered by the elements, sometimes completely disappearing from view. I sobbed against a rising conviction that any moment Adam would be swept overboard and lost forever.

Then I saw that he had climbed up to the lifeboat. Just as he reached out for the boy, a wave rose like a giant hand and engulfed them.

My prayers were sobs caught in my burning chest. *I loved him.* The knowledge was no longer something I could deny. I could not hold back from a truth that had been there from the first moment his lips touched mine.

My eyes were fixed upon the spot where they had disappeared.

The foaming wave washed away. They were no longer there. The lifeboat was an empty silhouette.

I was about to slump to my knees when my vision cleared. I saw them. Thank God, I sobbed. They had safely reached the deck and Scotty's arms were wrapped tightly around my husband's neck as they came toward me.

"Adam . . ." I sobbed. His bravery had crystallized feelings that I would have denied under any other circumstances. The shock of seeing him nearly swept to his death had forced me in one terrifying moment to accept the truth. Even though I loathed his manipulation of me and could not understand what demon drove him, I could no longer fight the spell he had laid upon my emotions. He had touched me on a level I never knew existed. I had fallen in love with Adam Demorest.

9

A very frightened little boy was put into his parents' arms. They thanked Adam profusely but he brushed their grateful remarks aside. "You should thank my wife . . . she's the one who found him hiding in one of the lifeboats."

"No," I protested, "you risked your life climbing up to get Scotty! And I . . . and I thought you were both lost . . . washed overboard." I could not disguise the tears flooding into my eyes as I went into his arms. "I was so frightened . . . so frightened," I sobbed against his chest. Both of us were dripping water all over the polished floor.

A group of people had formed around us and I could still hear the party merriment going on in the Grand Salon. A grotesque mob in costumes and masks pressed close to see what was happening. As my eyes fled over them, I looked for the black monk and cowered close to Adam. Someone brought a blanket and draped it over my shivering body.

"Come on . . . let's get you into some dry clothes—"

I didn't think I would ever be warm again. Hot water bottles and heavy covers had little effect upon my chattering teeth and the icy shivers going up my back. I knew that shock was a part of my bone-deep chill. My emotions were so fragmented that I couldn't control them. I wanted to laugh, cry, swear, and sob, all at the same time.

Adam held a glass of brandy to my blue lips and the fiery liquid sent warmth sluicing down my throat. He had taken off his own wet clothes and sat on the edge of my bed wearing a maroon quilted dressing robe. His hair was still wet and tumbled down his forehead. I wondered why I had ever thought him fierce and uncaring. He had risked his life to save a little boy. I would never forget that moment when I thought the sea had swept him away from me. He had been equally concerned about me . . . especially when he heard about the attack on Jasper.

"Is Jasper all right—?" I asked.

He nodded. "The ship's doctor says it's not serious. I'm just glad he was there—" He brushed back my hair and stroked my cheek in a tender caress. "We'll talk about it later. You've had enough emotional trauma for one night. Now get some sleep. Everything will look better in the morning." He stood up, bent over and kissed me lightly on the mouth.

"I'm . . . c-c-cold." Tears started easing down my cheeks.

"More brandy?"

I shook my head.

"More blankets?"

"N-no."

"What then?"

I reached out and took his hand. "Don't . . . don't go."

He sat down on the berth again. "It's all right. Nobody's going to harm you, Charl. You're safe with me."

"I know." The simple answer said so much. It was irrational—without foundation—and yet it was true. Whatever the conspiracy might be . . . he was going to protect me. "Stay here . . . tonight."

My request surprised him. One of his dark eyebrows rose. "What are you saying, Charl—?"

"I'm saying that . . . that . . . you . . . you could . . . come to bed . . . and keep me warm." My boldness surprised me.

He stiffened. "Are you trying to test my will-power? If you are, forget it. I don't have any . . . not with you lying there, so beautiful and entrancing . . . your lovely body so soft and supple—Good God, Charl, I'm a man, not a saint—"

"And not a devil, either. Or if you are it

doesn't matter anymore. I can't help how I feel. Tonight, when we were dancing . . . you were making love to me with your eyes . . . I knew it . . . and I couldn't turn away from it. And then when I saw you risking your life for Scotty, I couldn't lie to myself anymore."

"You may feel differently in the morning. You are under stress. You've had a traumatic experience—two, in fact. You're not thinking rationally."

"Yes, I am. For the first time, perhaps. It doesn't make any sense . . . but I love you." The words came easily. I spoke the truth. "I don't want you to leave me—" I wanted him to hold me, shut out the coldness, and share the strength that was in that tensile body of his. I wanted him to share my bed, hold me close, and make love to me. "We're legally married, aren't we?"

He gave me that rare, wonderful smile. "Would it matter, Charl?"

"I . . . I guess not." Social conventions didn't have anything to do with the way I felt about him.

His searching eyes never left mine. "There won't be any going back. It's taken all my will-power to keep my distance from you as it is. Darling, do you know what you're doing?"

"Making indecent advances toward my husband?" I answered lightly.

He lowered his head close to mine, his blue-gray eyes searching my face before he lightly kissed my eyelids. "And you know he's not one to turn them down—"

"Are you going to quit talking . . . and come to bed?" I demanded in a wifely tone that made both of us smile.

I was suddenly very frightened—not of him but of my own ignorance. I knew nothing about consummating the love rising in me. I knew that I wanted him in a way that was bewildering and wonderful.

He untied the sash of his robe and let it drop away. His male form was worthy of a Michelangelo statue—firm, smooth, with well-toned muscles molding a beautiful physique. He could have worn the clinging tight pants of any cavalier costume for the masquerade. They would have shown off the male form at its best. But I was glad he hadn't. I felt foolishly possessive about him.

He slipped in beside me. As if he knew my trembling was not entirely from being cold, he held me quietly, very gently kissing my forehead and stroking my hair. He made no swift movements or bold advances but let the warmth of his body ease into mine. I could feel his long, virile frame through the soft fabric of my nightdress. It was a wondrous sensation, this physical contact, this routing of loneliness. A unique sense of belonging in his arms took me by surprise.

"I love you—" he whispered, tugging at my earlobe as if tasting its sweetness. "You don't know how many times I wanted to push open your door and take you in my arms like this. The first time I saw you, you taunted me with your loveliness . . . your sunrise hair and the ivory smoothness of your skin."

I raised my arms and circled his neck, delighting in the way my breasts pressed against his bare chest. I need not have worried about my inexperience. He led me slowly and deliberately step by step. He kissed me gently at first as if coaxing warmth back into my lips. Then the pressure deepened and he kissed me again and again until my mouth was soft and pliable and became an extension of his own. Warm and supple when my lips parted to receive his questing tongue, a shiver of delight went through me and I felt a spiraling of pleasure throughout my body.

Then he slipped off my gown. I was no longer cold but radiating a mysterious heat that came from within. I had never been naked in bed before and had never been conscious of the sensual delights it offered. His hands traced the yielding curves of my body and as I lay naked in the circle of his arms, his mouth found the rosy tips of my breasts. Instantly a spiral of pleasure radiated from nipples that mysteriously hardened under his flickering tongue.

A murmur of pleasure escaped from my lips. It was bewildering, delightful and all-consuming. Delicious quivers went through my body. I crossed a leg over his and let my hand mold the hard sinews of his back. My fingers tingled with the touch and I was caught up in a need to stroke and feel and press him closer and closer to me. Marvelous, incredible sensations stirred within me. My breathing was rapid. I wanted him to appease an overwhelming hunger. When I arched against him with a need to feel every inch of his body against mine, he swept my legs apart.

There was a moment of suspended, bittersweet pain and then a splendor of unbelievable magnitude as he thrust into me. I had never imagined such a powerful experience. "I love you . . . love you . . . love you—" he whispered, carrying me away with the rhythmic possession of my body. I didn't want it to end and when my body suddenly burst with an awesome sensation, I gasped in surprise. When he slipped away from me, I felt a moment of regret. Then I realized that his lips were on mine in a gentle questing that held another promise of a complete and perfect oneness.

It seemed to me that we made love as if the experience belonged to us alone. I discovered a passionate nature within me that had until now lain dormant and undiscovered. No one had touched it before. No wonder I had refused to consider Randell as a possible suitor. I must have sensed that love between a woman and a man should be an all-encompassing experience. I had not intended to fall in love. Every rational part of my mind had rebelled against it but nothing seemed more important than the fact that I had found the man who could take me to such physical heights.

The honeymoon which had been a pretense became a reality. We stayed in our rooms all the next day, eating, sleeping, and discovering the uniqueness of each other. I believed him when he said he loved me. In spite of everything, the trust was there. We talked about the terrifying incident in the storm.

"I couldn't believe my eyes when I saw you out in that watery holocaust," he said as we enjoyed a very late breakfast the second morning. "I had been all around the ship and was about ready to give up. If you hadn't seen Scotty—"

"The little fool was trying to climb down. I told him to stay where he was. I was going for help—"

"There's wouldn't have been time," said Adam, shaking his head. "He'd have been washed overboard."

"I thought both of you were gone. That last big wave—"

"I know . . . but we made it down all right. That's all that's important." He threaded my loose hair in his fingers. "I'm almost glad it happened—"

"Almost?" I teased.

He did not return my smile. That careful, feline wariness was in his eyes. "Let's talk about what happened in the corridor. Jasper told me that he was seeing you back to your room and you were attacked.''

I nodded, closing my eyes a moment against the memory of Jasper slumped on the floor with blood running down his face. "We were coming down the hall. Jasper insisted that I wait for you in my stateroom. Suddenly there was this masked, hooded creature dressed like a black monk behind us. He hit Jasper with a wrench, dropped it, and lunged at me. Luckily, Jasper was able to grab one of his legs and that gave me a chance to get away.''

"He said it was a man's leg. But he couldn't tell anything else because of the heavy black robe.''

"I screamed but I guess nobody heard me— probably because of the storm. Anyway, Jasper shouted at me to run—and I did. The attacker was almost upon me when I reached a door leading outside. I dashed out into the storm, fearful he would follow me—but he didn't. I clung to a brass railing as the wind, rain, and surging waves tried to sweep me overboard. Then I thought I heard a child's cry! I called Scotty's name and I made my way down the deck until I came to the lifeboats. . . . Then I saw him.'' I shivered. "The whole thing's a nightmare. Why would anyone want to attack me?''

Surely the time for answers had come. He would be honest with me now. Whatever deceit that lay between us must be brought out in the open. I felt that I could face anything if only he would be honest with me.

But his eyes were shuttered. He shook his head. "I was afraid that something like this would happen. Do you think it could have been George Haversham?"

"I . . . I don't know. Yes, I suppose it could have been him. I didn't see him with Maudy . . . but, of course, he could have been there in costume and I might not have recognized him. But why? Why on earth would he do such a thing?"

He covered both of my hands with his. His probing gray eyes searched my face. "Tell me about Cousin Della . . . and the plans she had for this trip."

"What is there to tell? She was going abroad and invited me to accompany her. I was delighted with the invitation. She'd never made such an offer before even though I had hinted many times I would love to go with her."

"Pretend that you are describing her to someone who's never met her," he coaxed.

"But you've met her—" My throat was suddenly dry. Cousin Della's half-finished letter came back and with it the rush of unanswered questions. I did not want to think about my lover's treachery. I wanted to close it out, keep it away from this happiness I had found. Selfishly, I clung to a hope that he would soon explain away all the mystery.

"So you've never traveled with her before?"

I shook my head. "No . . . but I wanted to. It seemed to me her life was exciting, full of new

Thrill to the most sensual, adventure-filled Historical Romances on the market today...

FROM ▉ LEISURE BOOKS

As a home subscriber to the Leisure Romance Book Club, you'll enjoy the best in today's BRAND-NEW Historical Romance fiction. For over twenty years, Leisure Books has brought you the award-winning, high-quality authors you know and love to read. Each Leisure Historical Romance will sweep you away to a world of high adventure...and intimate romance. Discover for yourself all the passion and excitement millions of readers thrill to each and every month.

Save $5.⁰⁰ Each Time You Buy!

Six times a year, the Leisure Romance Book Club brings you four brand-new titles from Leisure Books, America's foremost publisher of Historical Romances. EACH PACKAGE WILL SAVE YOU $5.00 FROM THE BOOKSTORE PRICE! And you'll never miss a new title with our convenient home delivery service.

Here's how we do it. Each package will carry a FREE 10-DAY EXAMINATION privilege. At the end of that time, if you decide to keep your books, simply pay the low invoice price of $14.96, no shipping or handling charges added. HOME DELIVERY IS ALWAYS FREE. With today's top Historical Romance novels selling for $4.99 and higher, our price SAVES YOU $5.00 with each shipment.

AND YOUR FIRST FOUR-BOOK SHIPMENT IS TOTALLY FREE!
IT'S A BARGAIN YOU CAN'T BEAT! A Super $19.96 Value!

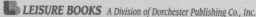

▉ **LEISURE BOOKS** *A Division of Dorchester Publishing Co., Inc.*

GET YOUR 4 FREE BOOKS NOW—A $19.96 Value!

Mail the Free Book Certificate Today!

Get Four Books Totally FREE— A $19.96 Value!

PLEASE RUSH
MY FOUR FREE
BOOKS TO ME
RIGHT AWAY!

Leisure Romance Book Club
65 Commerce Road
Stamford CT 06902-4563

AFFIX
STAMP
HERE

people and new places, while mine was dull and stagnant. I think my father must have suggested that I accompany her to England this spring. I'd been out-of-sorts and restless all winter—hard to live with, I guess," I admitted sheepishly. "Anyway I jumped at the invitation . . . and was delighted that she wanted me to come with her. She did all the planning. I don't even know what our itinerary was—where we were going or how long we were going to stay." I saw the furrows in his forehead deepen.

"She didn't mention any people that you might be visiting?"

"No."

"No specific tourist sights she wanted you to see?"

He sighed as I shook my head again. "You're very fond of your cousin, aren't you? Loyal to her?"

I assured him that I was but on some level I knew I had already betrayed her. I was in love, bemused, unable to control my own feelings. "Please tell me what happened to her."

"She hasn't been harmed."

"Then why . . . why force me to accompany you like this? Why threaten my father?" Suddenly guilt feelings overwhelmed me. Cosseted in my newly found love, I had forgotten about my father and about Cousin Della.

"Something is at stake here that is bigger than your cousin . . . and I didn't expect anyone to be aboard who knew her. It presents a problem I didn't foresee."

"What has she done?"

I think he might have answered me if a knock at the door hadn't changed everything. It was Jasper and he whispered something to Adam which I could not overhear. I saw Adam nod, close the door, and then turn back to me. I thought his smile was rather forced.

"Jasper brought a message. We're expected for lunch . . . with the Lynwoods. I guess the Professor has been missing us."

"Do we have to go?"

"I'm afraid so. Apparently our absence has been noticed." He kissed me lightly on the forehead. "We'll continue our conversation later."

"Promise?"

He nodded but I felt that I was being placated like a child who asked too many questions and was being put off.

When we entered the dining room, both Adam and I stopped in amazement and confusion as a round of applause greeted us. Everyone was smiling and all the men stood up. Scotty's parents beamed as the Captain came forward to meet us. I realized then that Adam was going to be honored as a hero.

Later I wondered whether or not he might have bolted if my arm hadn't been through his. I felt him go rigid and his expression was more than just surprise, it was one of protest, almost tinged with anger. He did not want to be in the limelight in this fashion. His jaw tightened and there was no softness in the smile he fixed on his lips. As we moved forward, he was forced to shake hands and accept a profusion of compliments from the grateful parents. He was then invited to sit at the Captain's table.

"It was my wife who found the boy," Adam protested. "She is the one who should be honored."

His gallantry only increased the flow of admiration that followed him across the room. I knew him well enough by now to sense a rising agitation. The only smile that reached Adam's face was when a contrite Scotty marched forward and delivered a less than spontaneous, "Thank you, Mr. Demorest. I will never do such a bad thing again."

Adam nodded and then winked at him. Instantly a boyish giggle shattered Scotty's contrite expression. I could not keep the love from my eyes as I watched Adam relate to the boy. Ignoring everyone else, he chatted with Scotty all through lunch and I was left to carry on the social amenities with the boy's parents and the gray-haired Captain.

After lunch we endured more handshaking. When the Havershams approached us, I moved closer to Adam. In the bright lights of the dining room, it seemed absurd to harbor any fear of these rather ludicrous-looking people. As usual, Maudy was made up like an overblown dahlia in bright shades of purple and her husband's stocky figure was made even thicker in a plaid jacket and trousers.

"My, my—saving the boy's life in the storm

like that. I do declare I never heard of anything so brave," she gushed. "While the rest of us were playing the fool, you two were out in that wind and rain."

"Did you enjoy the masquerade, Mr. Haversham?" I asked pointedly, ignoring the warning pressure of Adam's hand on my arm.

"Not my kind of thing," he said readily. "But Maudy wanted to go."

"Didn't you think he looked marvelous in his costume?"

"What was it? I've forgotten."

"A magician—he even had a black hat with a fake rabbit in it. Entertained us with some card tricks, too. It was a great party. Too bad it was spoiled for you two."

"Do you know who was parading around that night in a black monk's costume, Mr. Haversham?"

I thought I saw a slight flicker in one eyebrow before he answered smoothly. "Can't say that I do. There were so many people there. You looked lovely in your Indian robe—"

Maudy gushed, "George and I commented that it was the kind of thing your cousin liked to wear. She was such fun. Too bad she's not here—"

"What did you say kept her from traveling this season?"

"I didn't say." Before I could make another comment, Adam maneuvered me past them and growled in my ear, "That was stupid. Why did you want to bait him like that?"

"Why not?" I flung my head up. "If he's the one, I want him to know that he'd better not try something like that again. What does he want?"

"Will you stay out of this, Charl! You don't know what the real situation is—"

"Only because you won't tell me!" I replied sharply.

"It's too dangerous—"

"For me to know . . . or to be kept in the dark?"

"That's something I haven't decided. Now smile. I told the Professor we'd join him for a drink."

Professor Lynwood loved to finish every meal with a brandy. The ritual was similar to my father's and I enjoyed being included. I was glad that he hadn't deserted me for the smoking lounge and I sipped a small glass of sherry while the men in our group enjoyed their brandy.

"Well, now, you two young people gave a good accounting of yourselves. I'm proud of both of you." Professor Lynwood beamed. "We were beginning to wonder if you had deserted us for the rest of the trip." I flushed and he only laughed knowingly. "We'll be in port in a couple of days. What are your plans then?" His eyes smiled under his busy gray brows.

Adam had never told me what was going to happen when we reached England. I looked at him and waited for him to speak.

He gave the Professor a rather embarrassed smile. "I have to confess that my thinking hadn't gone much past the honeymoon trip. I suppose we'll do the tourist thing . . . Charlotte has never seen London."

"You must take her to the Tower of London. Big Ben. Buckingham Palace. Westminster Abbey. Regent's Park. And, of course, she'll want to see Oxford. Her father would never forgive her if she missed that." That was the cue for the Professor to chat about the days when he and my father were students there. I saw a glimmer of pain in the reminiscences and I knew that he had expected life to turn out differently for him. A few years ago he had been a respected and famous scientist, wooed by the United States to conduct important experiments. Now he was returning home as a failure, accused of wasting the fifty thousand dollars that Congress had paid him. I reached over and squeezed his liver-spotted hand. "I know my father values those days as much as you do."

He looked at me gratefully. "And, of course, you must come and visit us at Lynwood Manor. It is located southeast of London . . . on the coast. Yes, you must come. It would give me great pleasure to have you spend part of your honeymoon there."

I hesitated and looked questioningly at Adam.

"Thank you, sir. Charlotte and I would enjoy that very much." He smiled warmly at me and squeezed my hand.

I could not keep the joy out of my voice. "My father will be so pleased." Maybe the nightmare would be over the minute we left the ship, I thought. The thought of seeing London with Adam brought its own flurry of excitement.

We talked about it as we walked around the deck after leaving the Professor in a gentleman's lounge. He loved to play cribbage and promised Adam a game when we visited Lynwood Manor. "And Charlotte will enjoy the gardens and rides through the nearby countryside," he had said.

"Sounds wonderful, doesn't it?" I said to Adam as we walked. How could anything darken our happiness if we were surrounded by loving friends?

All evidence of the storm had passed. The sun was warm and cheery, matching my effervescent mood. There were no clouds in the blue-white radiance of the sky—nor in my heart.

When we returned to our cabin suite, we made love again. This time Adam undressed me while I was able to enjoy every tantalizing stroke of his hands and feel his soft kisses as the garments fell away. Afterwards we slept and then he left me to freshen up for dinner.

I bathed, standing naked in the small lavatory and sponging myself with water from the tall folding washstand. My skin seemed glowing but a little rough as if the wind and sun had dried it. I had never been one to use many toiletries but I drew Cousin Della's out of her suitcase and applied some sweet-smelling rose water and glycerin to my face. Then I opened the bottle of green bathing oil and put a few drops into my hand. Something quite different from just green oil came out.

I stared at the cluster of green stones. Emeralds. Beautiful emeralds hidden in the green liquid sparkled back at me. My heart suddenly began to race. Bewildering thoughts spilled over each other. My Cousin Della had carefully chosen an ingenious hiding place for the jewels. Emeralds. Concealed in the bottle of bath oil.

I knew I had to think, calmly and logically. I wrapped a robe around myself and sat down on the edge of the bed and stared at the jewels which had to be worth a fortune. I was heartsick. The rumpled bed still warm from our lovemaking mocked me. Was this what Adam had hoped to find before the ship had crossed the Atlantic? Only his mistake of confusing my cousin's luggage with mine had kept him from discovering this hidden cache of jewels.

I went over everything that had happened. He had been very upset when the Havershams appeared on the scene. He must have feared that they knew about the jewels. It was obvious that they were unduly interested in where my cousin might be—as if they had expected to meet my aunt aboard. Maybe Adam thought I was going to deliver the jewels to them . . . and he had married me to make certain that he could control my behavior, even to the point of making me fall in love with him. He had questioned me repeatedly about Cousin Della. *He knew she was smuggling jewels!* I was positive of it. What a fool I'd been. What a lovesick fool. I sat there for a long time like one struck by sudden pain.

"Are you about ready, darling?" he called from the sitting room.

His voice brought me back to the moment.

"No . . . not quite," I stammered. Hastily, I poured the jewels back in the bottle and had just tightened the lid when he came in.

"Need some help?" He was already dressed in an evening frock coat, black trousers and gold cufflinks sparkling on his white linen. His shiny black hair gleamed in soft waves.

"No, I was just putting on some lotion."

"Hmmm, smells good. What is it?" He nuzzled my neck.

"Rose water."

"Such nice soft skin . . . Next time call me and I'll do it. I'm a very good back-rubber. Want to give me a try or would that just lead to our being late for dinner?"

I did not return his flirtatious smile.

"What is it? What's wrong? Aren't you feeling well, darling?"

I walked away from him and set the two bottles on the highboy. Then I turned around. "Cousin Della has been using her travels to smuggle contraband, hasn't she?"

I had the satisfaction of seeing him start—as if I'd unexpectedly thrown water in his face. "She's a smuggler. You might as well admit it."

"Yes, but how—?"

"How did I know? Maybe I've known all along," I taunted him. "Maybe I've been playing you for a fool."

The color drained from his face.

"What are you talking about?" His voice had that wintry, sharp, cold edge.

"You and the Havershams aren't as smart as you think you are. My Cousin Della has outwitted you all." I began to laugh and laugh hysterically—until he reached out and soundly slapped my face.

10

Dinner was a stony affair. I had come only because I didn't want to be shut up in our quarters with my captor. My outburst had caused Adam to try and make me talk . . . but I had refused. After he slapped me, I withdrew into a cold, defensive silence. The more he threatened or cajoled, the tighter I set my lips. I refused to say any more.

Pamela noticed the change between us right away. "You don't look well tonight, Charlotte," she remarked, as if delighted in the way I was giving my bridegroom an "Ice Maiden" treatment. My father used to call it that. Whenever my temper was raging hotly on the inside, my attitude on the outside was correspondingly frigid.

The Professor seemed concerned. My behavior was such a sharp contrast to the lovesick bemused bride of that afternoon that he matted his gray eyebrows in a deep frown. He was too well-bred to come right out and ask what had happened. He reached over and patted my hand reassuringly. How could he know that my whole world had turned upside down when those emeralds poured out in my hand?

Larry asked, rather hopefully, "A lovers' tiff?"

"The course of true love never did run smooth," quoted Adam with a charm that caught a sob in my throat. Everyone laughed and Freddy winked at me in a knowing manner.

My husband made our present mood a casual, amusing thing. I wanted to leave the table in tears but stubborn pride made me flirt with Freddy just to infuriate Adam. I pointedly gave my attention to Larry who seemed to be both delighted and confused. I rather suspected it was true that this uncertain young man had a crush on me and in my present mood I was unscrupulous enough to capitalize on it. He was a nice person and at the moment I needed someone nice and sane to talk with.

"My father tells me you newlyweds have agreed to visit us," Larry said, his plain face brightening. "What a pleasure. Do you ride? We have a wonderful stable. While my uncle has been in the United States, I have added ten new mounts of the finest horseflesh in the county. I have just the perfect little sorrel mare for you."

"She would have to be pretty gentle to match my skill," I confessed. Most of my riding had been on a rented mount in Fairmount Park which provided numerous bridle paths along the Schuylkill River.

However, Adam brightened considerably. He immediately engaged Larry in an animated conversation about horseflesh. I remembered then that he had confessed it was one of his passions. *Along with jewels, no doubt!*

I closed out the rest of the conversations, my mind filled with questions. What should I do now? The revelation about my Cousin Della's illegal activities had shaken me. It must have been going on for years. Probably she and her husband had begun thwarting the law when they traveled together while he was in the service and after his death, she had continued. Hiding the jewels had obviously been an effort to deceive someone—Adam and the Havershams? All thieves together! My cousin had always been so special and my sudden disillusionment was a wrenching experience. In spite of the evidence, I wanted to deny that the wonderful, exciting cousin whose life I had viewed with envy was a smuggler. There must be another explanation. Perhaps she had just put the emeralds in the bottle for safekeeping. I knew that she was eccentric enough to ignore the ship's safe and hide her cache in a creative way. She might have had a bill of sale for them and planned to have them set into jewelry when she arrived in London. Yes, that must be it! Why should I assume that she had no intention of declaring them? Why should I assume they were contraband?

I must have changed expressions because the Professor leaned over. "Are you feeling better, my dear?"

"Yes, I am. I . . . I must have been hungry."

"You do have a rather unladylike appetite," commented Pamela, rather smugly, always sending a nearly full plate back to the kitchen.

Even in my distress, I managed to clean mine. Pamela's gaze lingered on my shoulders and firm arms as if I was carrying too much weight for her taste. It was true that my figure was more rounded than her angular, tall frame.

"Charlotte doesn't need to peck at her food in order to keep her lovely, feminine shape," countered her brother. "You'd probably look like Queen Victoria if you let yourself go, Pamela."

"And look who's talking!" she snapped. "Your middle disappeared long ago."

"That's enough squabbling. Your manners need some attention," countered the Professor rather sharply. "I hope, Pamela, that you have engaged a good cook at Lynwood Hall. None of your ascetic meals—I want our guests to be well-fed."

"We are going to have a houseful," complained Pamela with a tight smile on her lips. "I've persuaded Freddy to visit us, also."

"I hope that my presence will not be an intrusion, Sir?" Freddy asked.

"No, no, not at all. I love to have the manor filled with young people," said Professor Lynwood. "We've always been noted for our hospitality. I've been grateful to my niece and nephew for keeping the place up while I was working on my experiments in Washington. It will be nice to get home again . . . and have all of you there with me." He lifted a champagne glass for a toast. "Tomorrow we touch English soil. Here's to good friends—on sea and land."

After we drank the toast, the Professor began to brag about Lynwood Manor. As the oldest son, he had inherited the family estate but from what I gathered, he had spent most of his life away from it. His studies and reputation as a foremost physicist had taken him all over the world—but it was clearly Lynwood Manor that he loved. Even as the Professor talked about his estate and all the things he wanted to show me, I knew that I would never see them. They were part of the tinsel world I had built around myself while I tried to ignore bitter reality. My emotional cocoon had been wrenched from me when I found Cousin Della's jewels.

Inside of me, some of the fury began to die and I knew that my impulse to thwart Adam was a foolish one. Withholding knowledge of the jewels would bring more pain than satisfaction. I had the means to end the charade. As I sipped the bubbly champagne, I knew that I could not go on with it. As soon as I placed the emeralds in Adam's hands, it would be over. He would have what he wanted; my father would be safe and I would be released from my commitment as hostage bride. We would go our separate ways and I could take passage on the first boat back to America. My life would be as it had been before. Even as I clung to this hope that everything that had happened would fade away like a bad dream, I knew it would not happen that way. I had known a lover's embrace and no matter how deep his treachery, I would never stop loving him.

I pleaded a headache as soon as the dessert cart was taken away and asked Adam to take me back to our quarters. Now that I had made my decision, I wanted to get it over with. Tomorrow we would leave the ship and I wanted to begin making plans for returning home.

"We have to talk," I said as he closed the hall door behind us.

"Well, that would be a welcome change," he said wryly. He tossed off his coat and sat down on the settee, leaning his head back against the cushion in his favorite, casual fashion. "I was beginning to think that cold shoulder was going to be a permanent state of affairs." He crossed his arms over his stomach in languid and relaxed manner. "What brought on this display of feminine hysterics, darling?"

"Don't *you* call *me* darling!" I snapped. "I'm

neither your 'darling' nor your 'wife' nor anything else."

He gave a sigh. "Charl, are you going to tell me what this is all about?"

"With pleasure!" I said very evenly and clearly, "I have what you want."

He jerked his head up. "You what?"

His expression of utter consternation brought a smile of satisfaction. "You do? How did you get them?"

"You weren't nearly as clever as you thought."

He got to his feet slowly, his eyes as cold and hard as tempered steel. "You'd better give them to me—now!"

"Maybe I will . . . and maybe I won't," I taunted, foolishly holding on to my sense of power.

He grabbed me by the arms and held them cruelly at my side. "We're not playing games here!"

I wondered how I could have ever thought his voice soft and tender. His voice matched his eyes.

"Where are they? How did you get them?"

"I . . . I found them. Now take your hands off me! You can take them and get out of here! I never want to see you again—never, never, never!"

He dropped his hold on my arms and I lurched away, blinking furiously against the angry tears filling my eyes. He followed me into my stateroom. When I reached up and took down the green bottle, his eyes fixed on it in utter bewilderment. He thought I'd lost my senses. My victory was very sweet.

"Hold out your hand!"

He did and his eyes widened as I poured out some of the green liquid—and the emeralds. The exquisite gems made a glittering heap in the palm of his hand.

"My God! How—?"

I gave a brittle laugh. "Cousin Della fooled all of you! The bottle was in her suitcase, sitting in the hall with her hatbox. The hackney driver must have collected them and put them with my luggage. They've been here all the time." My gloating laugh was brittle. I couldn't help but turn the screws. "You weren't nearly as smart as you thought you were. Now you can take them and get out of my life!"

"Shut up and let me think." He turned away from my tearful, gloating face and walked back into the sitting room.

As I followed him, I brushed away hot tears. This was my moment of victory and release. He was not going to take it from me. "You and the Havershams can fight over them now. May the best smuggler win!"

"For God's sake, Charl, be quiet!"

"No. It's my turn to tell you how abominable you are! How I hate you for using me! How I loathe you for the selfish, heartless person you are." I choked on my own sobs. "Take the jewels

—and get out of here. When I get back home, I'd better find my father in perfect health—"

He sat down again on the edge of the settee and stared at the jewels. "Of course, that's what George Haversham was after!"

"Just like you! But you were ahead of him. You were the one who arranged for Cousin Della's 'accident' and took me hostage! No wonder you weren't pleased to find the Havershams aboard, asking for my cousin!"

He ignored me.

I sat down, my knees weak. What was the use? My spurt of defiance and anger was spent.

"The Havershams thought Della had given the emeralds to you," he said in a slow, even tone, like someone carefully sorting out his thoughts. "What a surprise it must have been when you showed up and Della didn't. They must have set up this thing while in Hong Kong—she was to get the emeralds out of the country and then turn the Havershams' share over to them. Or maybe they had already paid her for 'services rendered' for getting them out of the country. When you didn't make any move to deliver them, George Haversham got impatient. He must have thought you had decided not to give them up." He stared into space as he talked. "That must be it. Desperate, George Haversham attacked you and Jasper, intending to physically force you to give them up." He raised his eyes and stared at me, as if a mental jigsaw puzzle were falling into place. "I was afraid they might have some connection with your cousin but I never expected anything like this."

His monologue didn't make any sense. He didn't act like a thief who had just put his hands on a cache of jewels. If anything, he seemed completely ill-at-ease and anxious; any jubilation was clearly missing. All my sense of triumph dissipated. I stared at him. My voice was cracked as I asked quietly, "You weren't after the emeralds?"

"Hell, no. I didn't even know they existed," he swore impatiently. "Don't you think I would have searched everything in the house if I had been looking for them—including the luggage in the hall!"

Yes, of course. He wouldn't have missed Cousin Della's suitcase and hatbox. They had been sitting there in plain sight all of the time. Everything else had been planned too carefully to slip up on something as simple as that. My thoughts reeled like wild bees, buzzing and scattering in all directions. Relief that he hadn't used me to get the emeralds was instantly followed by an apprehension as sharp as nettles. *What did he want from me? If not the jewels—what?*

I felt myself trembling as the stark realization hit me—the charade was not over! He was not going to set me free when we reached port tomorrow. My emotions were so tangled I could not sort them out.

His words washed over me until he raised his voice. "Charl, are you listening to me?"

I nodded, blinking as his anxious face came into focus.

"There's only one thing to do. You'll have to give the emeralds to George Haversham—just the way your cousin had planned to do. I suspect that Della must have already been paid to smuggle the emeralds out of Hong Kong. Tomorrow morning, before we dock, you will make a present of that bottle of green oil and its contents to the Havershams—"

"No!" I looked at him horrified. "I won't do it. I'll turn them over to the authorities."

"You will not!"

"You can't make me involve myself in something like this!" Anger cut through my muddled thoughts.

"It will be all right—I promise you."

I laughed bitterly. "You promise? Well, any promise of yours should be very reassuring to me."

"Cut the sarcasm. You'll have to trust me in this."

"Trust you! I could go to jail! If the emeralds are contraband, I could be an accessory by giving them to anyone but the proper officials. Or end up like Cousin Della—what did you do to her? I know she was frightened . . . in the note she wrote to me—"

"Note?"

I jutted out my chin. "Yes, note. I found a letter she had started to me, telling me that she didn't want to involve me or my father—" I swallowed. "She had intended to send it to the

station to warn me—but she didn't have time." I
covered my face with my hands then. "Why are
you doing this to me?"

He moved quickly, kneeling down in front of
me and taking my hands away from my face.
"I'm going to protect you, Charl. I love you. You
have to believe that—"

"How can I? Why don't you give all of this
up—?"

"Because I have no choice." His mouth
tightened. "And neither do you, darling. You
have to do as I say."

"And if I don't—?"

"Don't make me threaten you. Please, just do
as I say. Tomorrow we'll leave the ship . . . and
enjoy ourselves in London . . . and then pay a
visit to Lynwood Manor. You would like that,
wouldn't you? By that time—" He let the
sentence trail off.

"Why are we going to London? What are we
waiting for? What is going to happen?"

"I'm not sure. We have to take it as it comes.
In some ways I'm as much in the dark as you
are."

The admission was less than reassuring.
Somehow I had come to depend upon his
autocratic confidence. I did not want to think of
him as a pawn in some intrigue not of his own
making.

"Someone else is telling *you* what to do."

"Yes. In some ways I have less of a choice
than you do."

"I'm frightened," I stammered, biting my underlip to keep it from trembling.

He pulled me up into his arms and I pressed my tearful cheek against his chest. His hands molded the curve of my back as he stroked me gently. "I know you are, darling. But you've also got enough courage to contain that fear. You'll do what has to be done. You'll do what I tell you."

I knew that I would give in but it was my nature not to accept someone else's authority gracefully. "I won't!"

"Yes, you will." He kissed my hairline with soft, tantalizing butterfly kisses. "In the morning you will go across the hall, knock on the door, and hand them the bottle. That will be the end of it."

"No." I raised my head and looked into his eyes. "That's not going to be the end, is it?"

His eyelids narrowed. "I wish it were. But I'm afraid that in some ways, it's just the beginning."

We did not sleep together that night. I think we both needed time to ourselves and some privacy to get ready for the events facing us the next day. He seemed to be wrestling with new problems and showing tight lines of stress around his eyes and mouth. I wondered what kind of power someone held over him. Was he as much a pawn in his bewildering intrigue as I was?

In a way I would be sorry to leave the Lucania. There was something reassuring about being at sea, in the isolation and protection from the rest of the world. A lifetime ago Adam and I had boarded the ship as strangers. Since then we had consummated our marriage vows in a way I had never thought possible and I was not the same person at all. How could I be that same restless, incomplete young woman? I had greeted the dawn in a lover's arms. Adam Demorest had brought me a fulfillment that I could not put aside. In spite of all my resentment and fear, I knew that I could not walk away from him no matter what happened.

The next morning I dressed once more in the green traveling gown which had been my wedding dress. My face was unusually pale and my hazel eyes seemed flat and lifeless. I conducted my morning toilette with a weighted slowness as if trying to put off the moment when I would have to emerge from my stateroom and set the day's activities in motion. Finally I could dally no longer. My steamer trunk had been repacked—everything was put away in preparation for our departure. I opened the door and found my husband waiting—with the green bottle in his hand.

Somehow he had replaced the green liquid and brought the contents up to full level. He handed it to me. "I wish I could go with you but it's better if they think you're acting on your own. I'll leave our door open—if there's any trouble, just yell . . . and I'll be there."

"What shall I say?" My lips seemed thick and dry.

"That Cousin Della wanted them to have this gift."

"What if they ask about her?"

"Be vague . . . say her plans changed. . . . Say she asked you to deliver the bath oil on the last day aboard. They aren't going to object. They'll have what they wanted."

"Are you sure? Maybe the Havershams are just what they seem—friendly travelers who knew my aunt. We don't know that it was George Haversham who attacked Jasper and me. What if it was someone else?"

He frowned as if he had already been over this ground in his own mind. "Then we will be throwing meat at the wrong dog!"

With this uncertainty echoing in my ears, he put firm hands on my shoulders and turned me toward the door. With faltering steps, I went across the hall and knocked on the Haversham's stateroom door.

"Come in! It's open," called Maudy and then opened the door before I could.

"Oh!" she said in surprise, her eyes widening and her smile uncertain. "I thought it was the steward coming to collect our baggage. Come on in, dearie. Georgie, look who's here. The blushing bride from across the hall."

Their sitting room was like ours but there was only one bedroom. As he came through the

185

door, I tried to assess his expression. There was nothing there in the bland face to reassure me that Adam had been right.

"Good morning," I said brightly, stilling the fluttering in my empty stomach. "I have something for you . . . from my aunt. I held out the bottle to him. "It's a gift. She told me to give it to you the last day aboard." I hoped the words didn't sound as much like a rehearsed speech to them as it did to my own ears.

Was there a slight flickering in his eyelids? Was he surprised by the peculiar gift of green bath oil? Or was he satisfied that my cousin had kept her part of the deal? I couldn't tell. I stood there like a statue, waiting for a cue as to what I should say next.

"Now, isn't that nice?" gushed Maudy. "Imagine that—Della remembering that we were going to be aboard and all! It's just too bad she couldn't come herself. What did you say happened?"

"Her plans changed," I said and thanked Adam for giving me the simplisitic answer. "Now I really must go. My husband is waiting to go up for breakfast."

"Will you be going on to London?" asked Mr. Haversham.

"For a few days, I think."

"You'll love it! Won't she, George? No place like it on the face of the earth. Of course, we won't be staying long ourselves—"

"Don't keep the girl from her breakfast,"

admonished her husband, patting his wife's fat arm affectionately. The unspoken message halted Maudy's chatter.

"Yes, yes, of course. Well, goodbye, dear—and best of luck to that handsome bloke you married." She winked at me. "Now that the honeymoon's over, maybe you two will get some rest." Her raucous laughter followed me out the door.

Adam was waiting for me. He shut the door and took me in his arms, holding me close to his chest. "How did it go?"

"Just the way you said—except—"

"Except what?" I could feel his body stiffen.

"Well . . . he seemed surprised by the gift . . . but . . . but I couldn't tell if it was because bath oil was a stupid offering under the circumstances . . . or whether he knew what he had in his hands."

He swore under his breath. "Well it's a calculated risk—and one we had to take."

The bustle of departing travelers from the Lucania brought its own kind of apprehension. We had said our goodbyes to the Lynwoods and had promised to visit them after a few days in London. I wondered if Adam really meant to accept the invitation or if he was just waiting to be told what to do next.

He allowed me to send a cable to my father. "Arrived safely. Will spend a few days sightseeing in London. All my love, Charlotte." I had wanted to ask my father to wire me in return but Adam crossed out the words.

"How do I know he's all right?"

"Because I say he is," was his infuriating answer.

We had just about passed through customs when Maudy's loud voice stopped me. "Take yer hands off me! You ain't goin' to push me around."

I swung around and saw that the Havershams had been taken into custody. A customs' officer held the bottle of green oil in his hands and two other officials held the Havershams captive between them.

My heart raced into my throat. *The customs' officer had found the emeralds!* Suddenly George Haversham pointed in my direction. "She's the one . . . she's the one who gave the bottle to me."

"Arrest her!" screeched Maudy. "The bloody little bitch set us up!"

Everyone's eyes turned in my direction. I felt my legs go weak. No, it couldn't be happening. It was a nightmare. In a minute I would be arrested and taken off to jail. My anguished eyes fled to Adam's face.

"Come on." He took my arm and swept me out of the building.

I shot an anxious look over my shoulder, certain that I would see a policeman bearing down on me. No one seemed concerned about our hasty flight. I could still hear Maudy's raucous voice raised in protest.

"Don't worry, darling," Adam reassured me as he hailed a waiting hansom. "The officials aren't going to believe anything those two say." A satisfied chuckle accompanied a slight curve of his lips.

I faced him, my eyes widening in disbelief. "You turned them in!"

"Yes," he said evenly. "They won't be bothering us anymore." Then he smiled at me. "Don't look so surprised, darling. Don't you know there's no honor among thieves?"

11

We were swept along in the crowd of departing voyagers, embracing friends and families united on the pier, and the bustle of hacks and drays collecting baggage. I let Adam take care of everything. Even when we were on the train heading for London, I could not dispel an overwhelming sense of unreality that mocked my arrival on English soil. Ordinarily, I would have been drinking in the landscape and all the sights that were speeding by the train window but instead, I sat woodenly with my hands folded in my lap, my eyes staring unseeingly ahead. The fear that had coursed through my body when I thought I was going to be arrested had left me weak and suddenly utterly exhausted. I would never forget George Havesham's accusing finger pointed at me. What if they were innocent? What if Adam had made me give the emeralds to an unsuspecting couple?

"It's all right," Adam assured me, sitting quietly beside me. His gray eyes took in my ashen face. "Don't think about it anymore."

I turned on him. "That's like saying, don't think about a purple, polka-dotted elephant," I countered. "It instantly brings that picture before your mind's eyes. Telling me not to think about the Havershams only makes the memory more vivid."

"True." He took my hand. "I'll try to give you something else *not* to think about. Don't think about being here in England—with all it's history, pomp and ceremony. Don't think about the pageantry, don't think about Buckingham Palace and Big Ben and—'" He continued pouring out word pictures which had the effect he wanted. They began to dim everything else but the excitement of being on a train heading for the greatest city in the world. During that short journey he kept my mind on things other than the scene at customs.

When we left the train that had brought us from Portsmouth, Adam secured a hansom for us. I had expected that we would register at some hotel near the heart of London but I should have known that the unexpected had become the ordinary. He gave an address on Regency Street which I assumed was that of a hotel. In spite of myself, a flutter of excitement overrode my apprehension and I enjoyed my first glimpse of London.

Horse-drawn omnibuses, hackney cabs, and regal carriages maneuvered for space in the crowded streets. Clerks, shoppers, merchants, nobility richly dressed and beggars poorly clothed surged along the crowded sidewalks. The sounds of jingling harnesses and clopping hooves mingled with those of a beggar's barrel organ and the cries of food and flower vendors hawking their wares from barrows lining the curbs. We quickly rode down broad streets which caught a feeble sun and I delighted in spring-green grassy parks and flowering trees which softened old buildings weathered by grime and age.

Soon we had entered a residential area filled with lovely Queen Anne and Victorian homes, newly mopped front steps and glistening lace-covered windows. Fenced-in grassy squares like small parks were dotted with nannies pushing baby carriages. I was startled when our driver stopped before a small residence set on a quiet square. I looked questioningly at Adam as the driver leaped down and opened the door.

"Whose house is this?"

"For the moment—ours," he said in that maddening calm tone of his.

"I thought we would be going to a hotel."

"This is more private."

And isolated!

I waited passively as our overnight bags were unloaded. Adam had arranged for the heavier luggage to be brought on a dray wagon. As he paid the driver, I wondered about Jasper. Was he inside, waiting to take up his duties as part-time jailer? My quiet exterior was at odds with an urge to run and scream and cry for help. My loving husband had become a stranger again.

At that moment a policeman in a high hard hat and blue uniform came strolling down the sidewalk towards us. Here was the law coming to my aid. Adam had readily admitted that he had handed the Havershams over to the authorities because it suited his purposes and I feared he would dispose of me in the same callous way when the time came. This was my chance. There would be no way Adam could avoid a scene if I decided to make one. I could rush toward the officer, pour out the story of my abduction, plead with him to save me and my father from harm. It was an opportunity I might never have again. The moment stretched into an eternity. I never knew what kept me rooted to the spot. No pleas for help came from my lips.

The officer tipped his hat. "Good morning to ye!" He said with an Irish brogue and a broad smile.

Adam returned the greeting and took my arm. The driver followed with our luggage. The policeman went on down the street and I looked up at the pale yellow brick house. It looked benign but I wondered if, when the white door closed behind us, it would become my prison.

Adam pulled a key from his pocket and unlocked the door. Then he turned to me and before I could react he had swung me up in his arms. "A bride should be carried over a threshold . . . even if it is a borrowed one." His touch was loving; his eyes softened with a caressing smile. My arms automatically went around his neck. I knew then that my love made me more of a captive than any prison.

He set me down inside a lovely white foyer. He tipped the driver, closed the door and drew me close again. I remained in his arms as if determined to reassure myself that there was nothing sinister or forbidding about the situation.

"Please don't look so frightened," he said softly. "There's nothing here to harm you." He bent his head and kissed me so passionately that it was easy to dismiss all my melodramatic thoughts as foolishness. "I love you, Charl," he whispered in a husky, passion-laced tone.

My own desires were fed by his hunger. Everything else faded into oblivion as his mouth covered mine, claiming it as his possession. The sweet taste of his parted lips and questing tongue drove all thoughts from my mind. The surge of sensations was so powerful that I could only feel—and not reason or protest.

"Come on—" he said huskily and drew me up the stairs. "We'll look at the rest of the house later."

There was no one in the house. We were alone. In a lovely Georgian bedroom, he pulled me down on the bed and shut everything from my sight except his loving, half-closed eyes as he kissed me again. My heart raced and I responded to his mesmerizing kisses and caresses. Every point of contact of his body on mine blazed with fiery warmth. My senses were filled with him—and nothing else. It was a new world, waiting to be explored.

When our clothes lay in a careless heap upon the floor, he pressed his nakedness upon me and I deliriously felt the sweet length of his chest, thighs and legs entwined with mine. He kissed my mouth and tasted the curve of my neck, moving with rapturous deliberateness to my breasts. Hard rosy nipples tingled as he took one and then another into his mouth, lightly flicking his tongue upon the sensitive apex. His breathing rose and fell with an urgency that was echoed in my murmurs. If I had thought that nothing would be as rapturous as the other times he had taken me, I was mistaken. He swept my leg aside and I arched to receive the thrust of his union. The exploding crescendo of our bodies uniting in rhythm was a peak that could never be lessened by repetition. There was no world but ours; no reality but exquisite sensation; no sound except breathless words of love pouring in my ears. We were swept upward to a pinnacle that exploded in a shimmering burst of bewildering delight.

Afterwards, we lay quietly. There was no need for words. Our passion had swept all other sensations away. I slept against him, content, fulfilled. Evening shadows crept into the room before we awoke.

I opened my eyes and found him raised up on one elbow, staring at me with a gentle smile curving his lips. "You sleep with the innocence of an angel—and with the lure of a seductress." He stroked my tangled hair, smoothing it over my shoulders, and capturing the unruly strands falling around my face.

His own dark hair lay in a rumpled mass on his forehead, softening the lean, hard plains of his face. His features were strong and yet gentle when he smiled, firm and yet loving when his facial muscles were relaxed. I reached up and touched his cheek, my fingers trailing over his smoothly shaven face. "I love you," I said.

"I know," he grinned with an infuriating smugness. Then he kissed my nose and nibbled on an earlobe. "Very tasty . . . but I think we'd better see if there's any food in this place. Unless you want to go out for dinner?"

I realized then that street lamps had been lit outside. We had made love and slept the whole afternoon away.

"How well does my wife perform in the kitchen?" he teased, easing off the bed.

"I'm not much of a cook," I confessed. "We have a reliable Irish cook, Mrs. O'Flannery, who won't let me poke my nose in her kitchen. 'A disaster, that youngun is!' to quote her. After several of my numerous culinary failures, the good woman gave up trying to teach me how to make bread or prepare a proper meal. As a result I've never improved on my first bungling attempts to bake or cook."

"Now you tell me," he said in mock indignation. He reached for his clothes and with a pang of regret, I watched that marvelous, lithe body disappear under smooth, tailored trousers and a soft white shirt. It thrilled me that his sensuous masculinity was an intimacy that I had experienced.

At that moment a musical doorbell echoed through the house disturbing my erotic thoughts. I immediately became tense.

"Relax, darling," he said, seeing my reaction. "It's probably the wagon from the railroad with our luggage." He leaned over and kissed me before he went downstairs.

I looked around the room then—nicely furnished, but with the same impersonal touches as a hotel room. No fire had been laid in the grate. No personal objects sat on the white mantel. Pictures in gilded frames were scenes of Regency Sound and were the only decoration on the pale blue walls. I had heard of "safe houses" and I wondered if this were one. A place to keep someone out of sight. I refused to let my thoughts wander down this dark path. Being here with him was the only reality my love-struck mind would accept. I deliberately closed off any other avenues. The warmth of his kiss had dissipated with his absence.

I heard voices going to the rear of the house and then the front door closed again. In the next minute he was back. "I had your steamer trunk put in a room downstairs. Since our plans are indefinite, you may not want to unpack it . . . just yet."

I didn't like the ominous interpretation which his words inspired.

He's waiting for something . . . or somebody. My mouth was suddenly dry. "What is going to happen?"

"I don't know. We'll have to wait and see."

"Why won't you tell me—?"

"I can't!" His eyes darkened to that flat, impersonal gray. "Try to relax, Charl, and enjoy your stay in London."

"Am I going to see any of it . . . besides this house?"

"Of course! You're not a prisoner."

"What am I then?"

"My wife." His tone was gentle. "Isn't that enough for the moment?"

"No," I said, but I lied. I, who had always prided myself upon my independence and clear thinking, had become a lovesick fool!

My fears that I would not be allowed to enjoy the sights of London were completely false. For nearly a week, we played the part of newlyweds who had nothing on their minds except to enjoy the wonderful sights of the City of London. We ate almost every meal in some picturesque restaurant, strolled along its boulevards, and took a boat trip down the Thames.

Pictures of Queen Victoria were everywhere.

Adam seemed to enjoy shopping in the exclusive royal shops and was so generous that we never returned to the house without our arms loaded with packages. I modeled the fancy lace underclothes with the teasing smiles of a harlot and then protested laughingly when he pulled me into bed. I dressed for him in lovely gowns which made me feel like someone pretending to be beautiful and seductive.

With my handsome and loving escort at my side, I twirled my parasol as we walked down Regent Street a short distance to Piccadilly Circus where a half-dozen streets converged. In the seventeeth century a "Piccadilly House" offered gambling and entertainment and the poet Sir John Suckling was reported to have lost his fortune there. Lord Byron had lived at 139 Piccadilly and had spent most of his married life on this street.

"How do you know that?" asked Adam, surprised at my command of trivia.

"My father is a Professor of Letters, educated in England, remember? I think I could find my way around London because my father has made it so real for me."

"Then I'm glad I brought my own private guide along."

He smiled and I said impulsively, "I'm glad too."

We tossed coins into the large fountain topped by a winged cupid statue and I wished that these wondrous days would go on forever. We wandered through the nearby shops and dined at the famous Criterion Restaurant. One evening we attended a concert at the Haymarket Theater.

We took a carriage down the Mall to Buckingham Palace and through St. James's Park. I loved Westminster Abbey. It was the most supremely beautiful church I had ever seen. For hundreds of years all the English kings had been crowned in Westminster on the sacred stone purloined by Edward the First. "He stole it and brought it here from Scotland."

"A royal thief," said Adam with a slight twitch at the corner of his mouth, surprising me with his own command of British history.

"Yes, you're in good company," I retorted but he did not rise to the bait. I was glad. Even though I had thrown the stone into the water, I didn't want it to demolish the contentment which we had found in each other's company.

As the halcyon days went by, it was easy to delude myself that we were just what we seemed, two people in love enjoying the sights of London without any overtones of mystery or deceit. Every day was filled with exciting excursions and every night with passionate lovemaking. The days sped by on golden wings —and then it happened.

Adam had taken me to see Hampton Court, a magnificent palace frequented often by Queen Elizabeth which I found as interesting as Buckingham Palace. Only the gardens were open to the public and as we walked through the exquisite, formal landscaped grounds, I tried to remember everything I knew about Hampton Court. "Shakespeare's play *Henry VIII* was acted there with himself as one of the cast. Did you know that?"

He looked amused as he shook his head and let me chatter on about how Queen Mary the First spent her honeymoon here with the dull, gloomy Philip of Spain. I was so enthralled with the sight of vine-covered turrets, the delightful smells of rosemary and hibiscus borders that I didn't sense Adam's preoccupation at first. When he took out his gold watch and looked at it, I realized that he wasn't really enjoying the garden tour.

"I'm sorry," I said quickly. "Let's call it a day."

"Are you tired?"

"I thought maybe *you* were."

"Well, maybe a little. How about a drive through Hyde Park?" he asked with a casualness that I was to remember later. At the time I accepted the suggestion without the slightest qualm.

From the moment we entered the huge park through Marble Arch at its northern end, I felt history bearing down upon me again for Hyde Park had been a fashionable meeting place as early as the time of Ben Jonson and literary references to it were numerous. Duels had been fought under the same spreading trees, I mused, as our carriage rumbled under the huge oaks. Coach races had caused many a mishap and unhappy women like Percy Shelley's first wife had drowned themselves in the Serpentine, a man-made lake at its center.

For the first time during our week of sight-seeing, Adam seemed to know what he wanted to see. "I've always thought I'd enjoy riding along the *route du roi*, now called Rotten Row. It used to be the route of kings from Westminster to the hunting forests but now it's only a bridle path," he said.

"You realy love horses, don't you?" I might have known that he would suggest a fashionable ride through the park. I steeled myself to protest that I wasn't properly dressed for such an excursion but he didn't suggest a ride. Instead we alighted from the hackney cab and he dismissed the driver.

Taking my arm, we strolled casually through the park until we reached a garden bench where we could watch the riders and their high-stepping mounts parade along the bridle path.

"Would you like something cool to drink?" he asked. "There's a small refreshment gazebo through the trees over there. Perhaps a strawberry ice?"

"A glass of lemonade would be refreshing," I conceded. The afternoon was warm and rather sultry for London and we had been going from one landmark to another without stopping. It felt good just to sit and loosen the streamers of my bonnet and let it fall down my back.

If Adam hadn't looked at his watch as he disappeared through a grouping of elm trees, I would never have thought anything about his absence. Somewhere deep within my consciousness, a bell went off. I stared at the place where he had disappeared through the trees. Why was he concerned with the time? He had never been before. In all our days of sight-seeing, I had never seen him look at his watch . . . until now. That was the second time he had taken out his gold pocket watch—in the garden at Hampton Court and now. Spears of sunlight hit my face and made me squint from the brightness . . . and yet I felt a chill on my neck. My indolent sense of contentment vanished. He had arranged for us to be at this spot in the park at a certain time. I knew intuitively what it meant. *He was meeting someone!*

Suddenly Hyde Park lost its charm. The heavy, dark green foliage was sinister. I felt alone . . . abandoned . . . vulnerable. All the apprehension and bewildering fear that I had been holding at bay came back. Adam had played the tourist with me, dallying away the days and filling my nights with a lover's passion. And all the time, he had been marking time. Tears as well as sunlight filled my eyes, blinding me.

Anger mingled with fright brought me to my feet. I tugged the streamers of my bonnet viciously as I retied them. Without considering the consequences of following him, I swept across the lawn toward the place where he had disappeared. I had to know. His pleas to trust him were suddenly jagged and sharp-edged like broken pottery. He had never stopped deceiving me. Even now my future was probably being considered by some stranger and Adam Demorest who had played me for a fool.

I came through the trees and saw the pretty gazebo which offered refreshments. He was not anywhere near the small structure. For a moment, I stood there, bewildered. Where had he gone? There was a cluster of customers getting ice cream and cold drinks and I walked purposefully a little way past them, looking in every direction, hoping to catch sight of the fawn-colored coat and light trousers which he wore that day.

My steps quickened and my eyes searched in every direction as I circled the area. I did not see Adam anywhere. There hadn't been time for him to go very far, I reasoned, finally turning back toward the bench where he had left me. Unless . . . unless someone had been waiting with transportation—like a horse or carriage. They could have ridden off to have a private conference.

There was nothing to do but wait. With my back stiff and nervous perspiration gathering on my brow I sat and watched mounted riders gallop along the bridle path.

It was fifteen minutes before he returned—with two glasses of lemonade. "What a crowd," he breathed, sitting down. "I thought I'd never get waited on."

How easily he lied, I thought as I took the drink, avoiding his eyes. If I hadn't known better, I would have accepted his explanation without question. His eyes slid to a mounted rider who was leading an empty horse on the bridle path. I stiffened and centered my stare on the man as he disappeared from view. The man was about Adam's age, I judged from his youthful build but I could not see his face clearly for it was shadowed under a jockey's cap. His clothes were those of a groom but there was a bouncing awkwardness in the way he sat on the saddle that belied any competence with horses. I sensed that Adam was watching me and I thought he tensed, waiting for me to say something.

It had all been done so smoothly, so professionally, that a soft-footed shiver climbed my back. The rider had been waiting for Adam with the extra mount. They had ridden a short distance together and then Adam had come back pretending he had been getting my lemonade. Even now, I wanted to believe that I had been mistaken, that there was another explanation. If he had not spoken then, I might have talked myself out of it.

"I've been thinking . . . that we've had enough of London for now. It's time to move on."

I held my drink with both hands to keep the sudden trembling from showing. *He had received his orders*. I jutted out my chin to give myself courage. "And where do you think we might go?"

"Why to Lynwood Manor, of course,"

I swung my startled gaze to his face. Why would he be taking me to my friends . . . unless . . . *unless he was through with me!* He was going to leave me. Whatever use I had been to him was over.

"What's the matter, darling? I thought you would be delighted. Once we get there, you can write your father. He'll be pleased to know you're visiting his old friend."

"And what if I don't want to go?"

"We can't stay here," he said in that flat tone of his.

I searched his face, trying to understand why someone else could tell him what to do. "Is it a matter of money? I haven't spent any of my vacation allowance."

"No, it isn't money."

"That house where we're staying must cost quite a bit," I pried.

"As a matter of fact, it was a generous loan."

"Then why can't we stay here . . . a little longer?" I was trying to buy time. I didn't want him to take me to Lynwood Manor and then disappear from my life.

"We'll come back to London another time," he said.

But I knew he was lying. There was no soft feathering of blue in his eyes.

My husband was preparing to sever ties of a mock marriage which had brought me such pain—and happiness.

12

We took a train south from London to a small village near the coast and then a five mile carriage ride to Lynwood Hall. It was spring in the English countryside. The weather was pleasant with a sky as blue as periwinkles. Men dotted the fields as they turned the brown, bare soil with ploughs usually drawn by a team of three horses, a boy at the head of the leader and the ploughman behind at the shafts. A flock of rooks and hedgerow birds followed the plough searching the clods for worms and grubs as they were turned up in the newly plowed earth. Fenced-in flocks of sheep filled the air with their melancholy bleats and found an echo in my own heart.

"Why are you so sad?" Adam turned my chin with his hand. "I thought you wanted to visit Lynwood Manor. And you'll be safe there—"

"Maybe I don't want to be safe," I said recklessly. "Maybe I want to be with you." I looked at him with my heart lurching like an off-balance top. "Please don't leave me there."

His black eyebrows rose. "What makes you think I'm going to leave you?"

"You'll do what you're told," I said flatly.

He gave a false laugh. "What makes you think I'm taking orders?"

I should have told him then that I knew about his secret meeting in Hyde Park but I was too hurt by his open deceit and was too proud to badger him. He would only tell me *what* he wanted—and *when* he wanted. I did not know what drove him but I feared it was an irrevocable force. He loved me. I knew he did—but I also knew that nothing I said would cause him to waver or change his course.

I sighed and turned to the soft English countryside and found some solace in the quiet serenity of thatched-roof cottages, half hidden by juniper bushes and copses of elm trees. Behind those whitewashed walls and diamond-shaped windows hardworking families shared their joys and sorrows . . . and at the moment I envied them. Donkey carts filled with produce from small allotments were bright moving specks along the country roads heading for the nearest village or hamlet which was easily identified by a church spire and a pub. A few buildings were scattered along the roadside, cloaked in greenery as if hiding from the eyes of the world.

ILLUSIONS

We alighted from the train at a small village near the sea and Adam hired a gig to take us to Lynwood Manor. As we bumped along a rutted road that skirted the gray-green water, I put my apprehensions behind me. It was a beautiful day and I was with the man I loved. For the moment that had to be enough.

I watched a flock of pelicans skim the water with the ease of floating feathers and let myself take in the panorama of sea and sky. Deep cliffs fell to the sea below and only narrow strips of sands that cupped the shore were suitable for walking when the tide was out. I could see fishing boats like dark flotsam dotting the waters and the smell of salt water, dank wood, and seaweed was brought to my nostrils on a brisk breeze.

"There it is," said Adam, pointing ahead. Then he gave a low appreciative whistle.

I don't know what I had expected to see, a small country house, perhaps, but the grayish-white stone mansion rising on a slight bluff at the end of a tree-lined passage was everything an Englishman's castle should be. It sat in the middle of its own ground, surrounded by small fields and dark copses which ran to steep cliffs along the sea. It was a very formidable, isolated structure and I had to remind myself that I would be with friends during my stay there.

"That's Lynwood Manor?" I asked in a hushed tone.

"Must be." He gave me a wry smile. "We're coming up in the world."

My stomach gave a peculiar lurch . . . as if somehow we were there under false pretenses. Even in the bright sunlight, I sensed a deep shadow lingering nearby. The front of the huge mansion was bold and austere, broken only by a wide double door which could be reached by a low flight of fan-shaped steps which stood on both sides of a wide terrace.

As I raised my eyes, three floors of windows gaped blindly at me. Overhanging eaves were elaborately decorated with creatures that looked like sea monsters. Slate-roofed turrets rising at each end of the enormous structure provided some relief from the structure's straight, unadorned lines. I could not see the sea now but I could hear it and as Adam helped me from the carriage the relentless pounding of water was like an orchestrated background to our arrival.

We mounted the steps and Adam summoned someone to the front door by a firm pull of a bell rope. "I wonder how many days it will take for someone to reach the front door," he quipped, smiling at me as if to ease some of the anxiety that must have shown in my face.

"It's almost as impressive as Broad Street Station," I agreed, trying to keep my voice even. How I wished we were back in the small house on Regency Street. We didn't belong here. It was wrong . . . we never should have come!

"It's going to be all right," he said gently as if reading my apprehension. "Just remember . . . we're on our honeymoon . . . nothing more."

"Nothing more!" I choked. He had used me for some nefarious purpose and I was supposed to pretend that I was a happily married woman looking forward to a life together—when everything indicated that he was going to abandon me at the earliest expedient moment.

"Adam, please . . . if you love me, take me away with you. You can't leave me here . . . I won't let you!"

"Charl—!" He gave a warning glance toward the driver of the rented gig who was waiting to unload our luggage. Adam's smile was still there but it did not reach his suddenly cold eyes. "You're going to have a nice visit with your father's old friend." He said it slowly as if instructing a child. His grip on my arm tightened in that familiar, warning manner. "Understand?"

I nodded. But I didn't understand anything. If the front door hadn't opened then I might have ignored all caution and given in to a rising hysteria.

Adam gave our name to a rather portly man who had opened the door. He wore servant's attire and his waist was an undetermined line on his protruding stomach encased in a black frock coat. Tufts of white hair sprang out from a balding head and matched a rather pompous walrus mustache. There was an authoritative air about him despite his rather comical appearance. His nod was questioning. "Good day."

"Mr. and Mrs. Adam Demorest. Please tell

Professor Lynwood we have arrived."

"Very good, Sir." Without smiling, the servant stepped back and waited for us to enter.

Our footsteps echoed on a gray-white marble flooring as we walked across a foyer and descended two steps into an enormous entrance hall. A high coffered ceiling brought my eyes upward to a magnificent glittering chandelier hanging by yards of gold chain above. A huge fireplace as tall as a man dominated one wall. Dark furniture of a size in keeping with the rest of the room included a rectory table flanked by royal blue, high-backed, throne-like chairs. A curved staircase mounted upward and a skylight over the landing sent a wash of sunlight down the plum-colored, carpeted stairs and polished oak banister and carved newel post.

As we followed the portly servant to the right into a small but elegant waiting room, my eyes darted from side to side, trying to take in all the lovely classical statuary placed in deep niches and valuable paintings that could have graced any museum. When the butler left us, I was afraid to move from the center of the elegantly furnished room.

"Wheee," said Adam, looking around. "You do pick your friends very well, darling. There must be several fortunes under this one roof."

A satisfied edge to his voice brought a sudden constriction in my chest. Horror as I have never felt before was like fire surging through my veins. Everything that had happened tumbled down upon me; bewildering events fell into a pattern for the first time.

"No," I gasped.

"What's the matter, darling?"

"You planned it all!" *The first, unexpected meeting with the Professor—and Adam's smiling friendliness. The way he had encouraged the Lynwood's company during the crossing. The ready acceptance of the invitation to spend part of our honeymoon here.* "This was your goal all along. You used me to gain entrance into this house!"

His eyes narrowed. "Don't let your imagination get away from you, darling." The order was a warning. "And remember . . . your father's well-being is still in your hands."

The reminder settled my hysteria. My voice was quite controlled as I repeated the truth. "From the very beginning you used me to get you inside this house!" I waited for him to deny it, prayed with all my soul that he would say something to prove me wrong. "It's true, isn't it?"

"Charl—"

"That's why you married me! You knew the Lynwoods would be on that ship! I was your entrance into Lynwood Manor. All along this was your plan."

His eyes flickered. "It's not what you think."

"And I was afraid you were going to leave me here." My laugh was brittle. "I was going to beg you to stay with me."

"For God's sake, Charl, quit trying to second-guess me."

"You're not going to get away with it."

"Get yourself under control." The command was quiet but with the sting of a whiplash.

"Yes . . . yes, I will. Perhaps for the first time! I turned out to be a willing pawn, didn't I? I fell in love and made everything easy for you."

"I didn't plan on that happening. You know I didn't. I tried to keep my promise—"

"But you're not above using my feelings to get what you want. Well, I won't sacrifice my friends . . . not to you . . . not to anybody!"

"Charlotte, listen to me. Nothing has changed." The use of my full name sobered me. There was nothing soft and loving about him. He had reverted to the calculating, determined, unscrupulous stranger. "The options have not changed. You either cooperate . . . or put your father in danger."

"You bastard!" I swore with choked breath. I had the satisfaction of seeing him wince.

"That may be—but you'd better continue the charade." He tried to touch me but I jerked away. Anger made his eyes a wintry pewter. "I'm warning you. Act the blushing bride, Charl, when we're in public. I'll leave you alone otherwise . . . if that's what you really want." He had the audacity to smile wryly at me.

"I detest you! You'll never touch me again!" If we had been anywhere else I would have picked up one of the French porcelain figurines and flung it at his head.

"The important thing is to convince the

Professor that we are happily married. Now compose yourself. You look like a shrew about ready to scratch my eyes out. Try to remember what there has been between us."

The memory of our passionate lovemaking was like sour bile in my mouth. How much of it had been deliberately planned to make me the lovesick bride? "You never really loved me," I taunted him.

"That's not true. I love you more than I should . . . and I wish I could change the circumstances, but I can't."

"Your accomplice in Hyde Park won't let you?" I asked sweetly, delighting in the widening of his eyes. "Oh, yes, I'm not as stupid as you'd like to think. I know you met someone there. You made the mistake of looking at your watch and I knew you were meeting someone. Pretty clever, going for a short ride so no one could overhear your conversation."

"Why didn't you say something?"

"Because I wanted to pretend that it didn't happen . . . that it was all my imagination. You must have been given orders to leave London and come here."

He did not deny it. I wondered then what he was after. It must be a great deal more than the emeralds he was willing to sacrifice to the Havershams. "What a fool I've been! I thought you were going to bring me here and leave me. Now I wish to God that I had been right. Please go." I touched his sleeve then, begging him with every ounce of persuasion that I could muster.

"I won't say anything. Just leave . . . now, before they come. I'll make up a story. I'll—"

"No."

Then we heard footsteps in the hall. Before I could react, he had pulled me into his arms and kissed me. He raised his head just as Professor Lynwood bustled into the room.

"What a surprise," he said, laughing at my heightened expression which he wrongly interpreted as embarrassment as I jerked out of Adam's arms. "When Winston told me you two lovebirds were here, I couldn't believe it. How was London? Did you see any of it . . . or did you find each other's company too absorbing?" He chuckled and I thought I was going to cry as I reached out and hugged him.

He shook hands with Adam. "Come along. We don't use the front of the house or any of these formal rooms except on illustrious occasions. The south wing faces the sea and those rooms are the ones used by the family . . . much more comfortable. I don't know where Pamela and Larry are at the moment. He's probably out in the stables. Got a mare about to foal. Pamela is probably in the garden with Freddy. Those two!" He shook his gray head. "Never thought I'd see my niece lose her head over any man the way she has over Mr. Heinlin. No accounting for love, is there?"

"No," I agreed with dry lips and forced a smile as Adam pressed a warning hand on my arm.

"Larry will be back in time for tea. That boy!

You'd think he was a royal prince the way he spends money on horses. Can't abide the things, myself. I'll take a bicycle any day. Maybe you'll join me in my daily spin, Charlotte? Bicycling is good exercise . . . and a great way to see the countryside."

"I'd love too." I disengaged my arm from Adam's and looped it through the Professor's as we walked down a stately hall. I was going to protect him. I didn't know how—or from what —but the cold stare I gave Adam delivered my message.

"Winston will have your things put in the gold bedroom—fitting for a bridal couple," said the Professor. "Of course, there's a small adjoining room if you two get in a spat. Never been married myself, but from all I hear it's a rocky enterprise from the beginning. I'm glad my brother did the duties and provided the family with some heirs. Well, here we are. Now, isn't this more comfortable?"

I couldn't see that the room was much smaller than one of the huge parlors we had passed. Four white pillars held up a vaulting ceiling decorated with moulding fashioned in intricate, baroque patterns. The walls were covered with tapestries that must have been worth a fortune. Gilded frames hanging from long gold ropes held numerous etchings. Deep pile rugs were scattered about on the polished oak flooring. If this was casual living, I feared I would never be up to any stately affairs.

The Professor led us across the room to a conversational grouping of two sofas and several easy chairs in front of a mammoth fireplace. A fire was burning even on this warm afternoon and I realized that the stone mansion must contain a perpetual chill. Through a row of mullioned windows, I saw that this part of Lynwood Hall looked out upon a terrace and green lawn sloping to the sea.

Adam took charge of the conversation, asking the Professor about the history of the house, and commenting on the beautiful landscape surrounding it. Winston brought in a tea cart and I sank back in one of the upholstered easy chairs and sipped the warm liquid gratefully.

When Larry came in, he gave a cry of delight and gave me a boyish hug. I could smell the faint odor of a stable upon his clothes. His uncle had been right about his whereabouts.

"What a nice surprise," he said. His round face was wreathed in smile lines. "I must confess that I never thought you would come. Not this soon anyway. Didn't you like London?"

"I thought it fascinating," I said honestly. "But there's too much there . . . to see at one time . . . and—" I floundered.

"We thought it would be a nice change to spend a little time along the coast," Adam finished.

"You made the right decision," said the Professor. "Southern England is beautiful! Now that I'm back, I wonder how I could have spent so much time away."

"I've been telling you that," said Larry in a

chiding manner. "But you wouldn't listen."

"What will you be doing now, Professor . . . to keep busy?" I asked.

"There's always work for a physicist. New ideas . . . new experiments."

"I'm glad the failure you experienced has not discouraged you."

"Discouraged, yes . . . defeated, no. I still have a few good years left in me. You haven't told me much about your father, Charlotte. Is he still the peppy, optimistic fellow he used to be?"

"Yes . . . he's still as outgoing as ever."

"And in good health?"

I swallowed hard, refusing to look at Adam. "I hope so." I was grateful that Pamela and Freddy came in and put an end to this painful conversation.

They must have been out walking. Freddy's blond hair was ruffled around his handsome face and there was color in Pamela's usually pale cheeks. Freddy greeted us with a broad smile and a welcoming, "Hello, again. Pretty as ever . . . England must agree with you, Charlotte. She looks great, doesn't she, Pamela?" He was as debonair as ever.

I could tell that Pamela was less than delighted to see me. Her welcome was quite perfunctory and lacked warmth. Obviously it was her uncle's home and she had to be gracious to his guests but she was the first one to ask how long we planned to stay.

"I really don't know—" I stammered, looking at Adam for help.

"Now, Pamela," chided her uncle. "Don't start worrying about that fancy party you're planning. There's plenty of room in this old place for dozens of house guests."

"Oh, I'm sorry," I said quickly. "Are we intruding? Is this a bad time—?"

"Not at all," boomed the Professor.

"The more the merrier," added Larry brightly. "Pamela's decided to open up the ballroom and have a homecoming celebration for Uncle Alex. That's what it is, isn't it, Sis?" he teased. "Not an engagement announcement?"

"Larry!" she retorted indignantly. Her angular cheeks colored.

Larry just laughed. "Well, I heard you asking for the family jewels to be taken out of the vault. Must be a pretty special occasion to get decked out in all those diamonds and rubies. I bet half the countryside will be here just to see them."

My hand trembled as I set down my cup. I did not hear the rest of the conversation. I sat there like an ice sculpture, not daring to raise my eyes and look at Adam. So that was it. Now I knew.

"You look tired, Charlotte," said the Professor. "I think you'd probably like to rest before dinner."

"Yes . . . thank you. I'm afraid I'm not very good company at the moment."

I waited until we were alone in the gold bedroom before I lashed out at Adam. "It's the jewels, isn't it? That's what you're here for!"

His expression was set in stone and he did not answer. He walked to the door of a small adjoining sitting room and surveyed a narrow day couch. "Well, I guess it will have to do unless—" he turned around and surveyed me and the huge, elevated four-poster bed. He raised a quizzical eyebrow.

"Don't even think it!" I flared. "It's bad enough that I have to be in the same room with you. Until this moment I never realized how close love is to hate. I can't stand the thought of you touching me ever again!"

"Nothing stays the same," he said in a sad, philosophical tone. Then he had the audacity to grin at me. "This, too, shall pass, my dear Charlotte."

"I am not your 'dear' anything." I knew I was close to bursting out in tears so I went into the spacious bathroom adjoining a narrow but elegant dressing room and closed the door. "I hate him . . . I hate him," I sobbed but I had never been much good at lying to myself. I could almost laugh at the incomprehensible fact that I was in love with a jewel thief.

I saw as little of Adam as I could in the next week. I found it easy to lose myself in the house and gardens. The Lynwoods let me set my own daily schedule and except for meals I felt no restraints upon my time. With a childish perversity, I would slip away and enjoy the gardens for hours at a time, take short walks in the nearby woods, or sit on the edge of one of the many fountains and let myself be mesmerized by the spray of liquid rainbows in the air.

Away from the house and away from Adam, I felt like a prisoner who had successfully escaped his bonds. He seemed to be willing to let me have a free rein. I refused to tell Adam where I had been or what I had done and I foolishly believed that I had outwitted him. This smug confidence was shattered one afternoon as I made my usual escape into the garden.

A dozen gardeners were always at work there, bringing spring plantings from the greenhouse, trimming bushes and cutting bouquets for the house. Impulsively I had volunteered to cut a rose bouquet for the rectory table and invaded the lovely rose garden, clipping a rainbow of long-stemmed, velvet buds just about to open.

"Good morning," I said as I came upon a gardener down on his knees mulching the base of a pale white rose. "Lovely day, isn't it?"

He lifted his head and I nearly dropped the basket of roses in my hand. It was Jasper!

For a moment, I couldn't speak. I blinked in disbelief, bringing that long chin and emaciated face into focus. There was no mistake. He was the same man who had driven me to Cousin Della's house the day of my arrival in New York. He had been my shadow on board ship. Now he was here. I had seen him dressed as a hackney driver, a steward, and now a gardener . . . pretenses, all of them!

He rose to his feet, his long face shadowed by a straw hat like those which I had seen on nearby farmers. His overalls were dirty and his garden gloves stained but I wondered how much of it was for show. I knew him for the impostor he was.

"What are you doing here?"

"Working—" He motioned to the mulched rose bed.

"I don't mean that!" I snapped. "What are you doing here at Lynwood Manor?"

His long jaw worked and I knew he had a chaw of tobacco in his thin cheek. He took off his hat and scratched his head. "Keepin' an eye on you, I reckon."

I knew then that I had not been alone for one minute in all my wanderings around Lynwood Manor. Either Adam or Jasper had me in his sight all the time. I felt sick to my stomach. Was there no end to the duplicity? Finding Jasper here should not have surprised me, I thought angrily. I had expected him to be at the Regency Street house. Never once had I suspected that he was already ensconced at the Professor's home. Adam and Jasper—two of them—waiting, planning and making certain that I did not interfere with their nefarious plans.

I was furious . . . and heartsick!

"How did you do it?" I demanded of Adam when I returned to the house. "I just met Jasper in the garden. It must have taken some planning to sneak him into the Professor's employment."

"Not at all. Jasper came around looking for work. It was as simple as that. I'm sorry if you were upset."

"Upset?" I echoed sarcastically. "Why should I be upset? I love being spied on every moment of the day and night."

"He did save you from Haversham's attack, don't forget."

"Only because he was protecting your investment. Besides, I'm not in any danger here—"

"Let's hope not."

"What does that mean?"

"Nothing." He clamped his jaw shut. I was certain Adam and Jasper were planning to steal Pamela's jewels the night of the party.

The nearby village of Downyville lay about a mile and a half up a straight narrow road from Lynwood Manor. The Professor and I easily traversed the distance on two sturdy Victor bicycles which boasted two wheels the same size, innovative pneumatic tires and frames capable of balance and speed. I enjoyed bicycling in Philadelphia but my Perkin's velocipede had three wheels and was quite unwieldy. My walking skirt was fortunately short enough to stay out of the way of the chains. I tied a bonnet on my head and let the wind whip my hair as I whizzed along the bumpy road beside the Professor, laughing and chattering. The accumulated tension which had made me short and curt with Adam faded away. I was with the Professor and I felt almost young and innocent again.

Everyone in the village knew the Professor. About a dozen cottages were scattered around a stone church and rectory, a small post office and several little shops. Rough-looking farmers tipped their hats politely as we passed and the Professor told me that most of them lived in a hamlet some three miles away. In the morning before dawn, they would throw on their clothes, breakfast on bread and lard, do their own chores, and then walk with their lunch pails three miles "goin' afield" to work another man's land. "My great-grandfather made his money in commerce; he came here and bought the Manor and raised a family. He was considered an outsider. It took two generations before the Lynwoods were accepted by the locals."

"But they must be proud of you now . . . your international reputation as an outstanding physicist."

"The outside world doesn't encroach much upon the daily lives of these people. That's why I came back—to get away from pressures in the United States and start anew after my bitter failure there. I was so certain that the blueprints for my man-size aeroplane were exactly right for a successful flight but—"

"What happened?"

"Crashed before the machine even became

airborne. A defect . . . I abandoned the experiments and came home—" He took a deep breath. "To this." He motioned around the quiet, rural landscape. "Makes the world and all its craziness seem very far away, doesn't it?"

"Yes, it does." Almost, I added silently. I loved being outside, breathing in the fragrances of wild flowers and grass. I enjoyed meeting new people, like the village blacksmith who stopped his bellows to exchange a few words of greeting with Professor Lynwood.

I posted a letter to my father which I had secreted away in the pocket of my long-waisted jacket. I had not written anything that Adam would have censored but it gave me satisfaction to post it without his knowledge. I wanted my father to know I was here at Lynwood. I wondered if Jasper were secreted someplace close by, reporting on my actions.

Something in my manner must have made the Professor ask rather abruptly, "Are you happy, Charlotte? Did your father approve of your marriage?"

"Why do you ask?" I responded with my heart suddenly leaping.

"Oh, I don't know. Sometimes you seem happy . . . and other times lower than a barge in the water. I don't know anything about love— old bachelor that I am—but sometimes your eyes look like a pup who's waiting to be kicked. Your husband isn't abusive, is he?"

"Oh, no—" I managed a laugh. I could have

withstood any rough handling—it was his tender caresses that I feared.

"I'm glad. You have character and moral strength, as well as beauty. You're like your father, Charlotte. I would trust him with my life. And I know I could depend upon you to do the right thing under almost any circumstance."

The bright sunlight suddenly paled. The day was no longer cheery and reassuring. His words held an ominous presentiment, like storm clouds gathering upon the horizon. "What do you mean?"

He smiled. "Don't look so worried. I'm just an old man chattering." He gave my arm a gentle pat. "Are you ready to start back? I'll race you to the first hedgerow." With that he was off with me left behind to gulp the dust from his wheels. I was unable to catch up with him despite my youth. The rest of the way we rode leisurely side by side and I was grateful that the conversation remained impersonal. I did not trust myself to lie to this dear friend.

I became fond of Larry Lynwood in a different way. He could have been the brother I never had and although I knew his feelings for me were more than brotherly, he always treated me as a married lady. He showed off his horses and we took some short rides along the water's edge when the tide was out. Once again the water and cool salt breezes had a healing effect and I could forget for a brief time the approaching party when everything would end for me.

Adam spent a good deal of time riding a big black horse which Larry had placed at his disposal. Midnight was the horse's name and I was warned that he would kick your head off if you got behind him. I thought Midnight and Adam matched each other. There was something wildly sinister and treacherous about both of them. And something fascinating too.

As I watched Adam kick the horse into a fierce gallop along the shore line, splashing the water like a demon in full flight, I wondered if Adam were releasing some pent-up anxieties of his own. His body was braced against the wind, his head held at an arrogant angle, and his horse whipped into a lather. I could not keep myself from worrying that he might be thrown. I chided myself for any concern over his safety but the night I had thought the sea was going to wash him away from me had not faded. That night became a recurring nightmare. Sometimes I woke up with hot sweat upon my pillow and his name on my lips.

I was glad that our suite was large enough to put some distance between us. We came and went like actors in a play, caught in a script that demanded certain dialogue and a predetermined level of performance. Adam insisted that we take some strolls in the garden to keep up the pretense of newlyweds wanting to be alone.

As we walked, I moved woodenly beside him, steeling myself against his touch and yet trying to give the impression of enjoying his company.

"Lovely place, isn't it?" he commented, breathing in the salty brisk air.

"Yes." I kept my eyes riveted ahead. "How long are we going to be here?"

"I don't know. Another week at least."

Pamela's party was a week away.

I wondered how many people suspected that our marital bliss was a sham. I knew that Pamela had a speculative glint in her eyes as she watched us. Fortunately she was so busy planning her party and keeping Freddy at her side that she didn't have much time or interest in further speculation. When she was busy or away from the house, Freddy sought me out. I found him to be as charming as Pamela was abrasive. His good humor and flattering flirtatious manner were a welcome change from Adam's calculated role-playing.

"I've been watching you in the rose garden, Charlotte," he said. "A perfect compliment to your beauty. You're the fairest blossom of them all."

I flushed and then laughed at the rather clichéd compliment.

"How sad that only your husband can enjoy your true beauty," he said, with a meaningful inflection. He lifted my hand and kissed it. "I wonder if he appreciates the treasure he possesses."

I didn't know how to respond. I'd had no experience with this kind of light, flirtatious dallying and even if I hadn't been married I would not have been capable of exploring such sexual quicksand. I quickly retreated from his suggestive remarks and turned the subject back to safe ground. He seemed amused by my naivete.

Sometimes Adam and I made a foursome with him and Pamela after dinner and played cards. Pamela seemed less prickly in Freddy's company but her possessive attitude toward him was almost pathetic. He seemed to tolerate it with good humor but did not change his behavior. He was the kind of man who could smile at a strange woman and make her blush from the intimacy of his glance. Even though I knew what kind of rogue he was, I was not impervious to his flattering smiles and winks. Undoubtedly Pamela thought she would be able to change him, I decided, but I was sure that he would make a terrible husband. I wondered why Freddy was courting her. Money, perhaps? But the Professor was only in his early sixties. It was likely Pamela would not inherit for many years. Could she keep handsome Freddy Heinlin on a leash that long?

One evening when we were in our rooms dressing for dinner, Adam brought up the subject. "I know you're trying to get back at me by flirting with Freddy but stop it."

"What conceit! I spend time with him because I like him. I enjoy *his* company."

"He's a womanizer of the worst sort. Stay away from him."

I was sitting at a dressing table with my back to Adam but I could see his face as he buttoned the front of his stiff shirt. "Are you playing the jealous husband?" I taunted. I wore a silk dressing gown he had bought in one of the Piccadilly shops. Adam had said that the sea-green satin was flattering to my white skin and greenish-gray eyes. At the moment they flashed with anger.

"I'd hate to see Pamela's claws bared on your face."

I snorted. "She might as well get used to it. Freddy's a very charming man; he makes a woman feel special. She'll never be able to keep other women away from him."

"Well, I know one giddy female who's going to keep her distance."

I laid down my brush and turned around. "You'd like to shut me off from everyone, wouldn't you? Keep me caged until you do your dirty work. Well, I like Freddy's company and if he decides he'd rather be with me than—"

With lightning speed, he jerked me up from the vanity stool. "You'll stay away from him," he growled.

"No," I gasped but the word was caught in my throat as his mouth pressed harshly against mine and kissed me insistently. For a moment my hand fluttered in protest against his chest but his arms were like steel bands around me. I could neither move nor breathe. Remembered passion sprang like dry earth suddenly coming to bloom again. The nights without him had been a torturous eternity. My pent-up desires burst free. In the next instant, he had flung me on the bed. There was no stopping the tide of desire that accompanied his angry, passionate assault and the fury of my response.

All my thoughts and protests were wiped out by the tempestuous intensity of his lovemaking. He rolled on top of me, his body heavy and demanding. His hands pulled my hips against the flaming heat of his loins and he took me with a savage thrust. Only when we were both spent and breathing heavily did I recover any semblance of control. Even then, I lay still in his arms and let the tears come. It was probably the last time I would ever lie in his embrace and be swept away by his love-making.

There was only one more night left before Pamela's party.

13

Like a child peeking at a grown-up party, I watched the arrival of carriages and fancy broughams drawn by sleek, spirited horses and reined to a stop by liveried coachmen. It was a scene out of a romantic novel and I would have thoroughly enjoyed it if I had not known the events that would destroy the light, frothy gaiety of the arriving houseguests. Winston was kept busy opening the front door and admitting fashionably dressed men and women of all ages. I had the absurd impulse to go down to the front door and order them away, as if this action might thwart the impending disaster.

All day Adam remained downstairs in the formal parlor, mingling with the new arrivals. I couldn't face anyone. I pleaded a headache, had breakfast brought up on a tray, stayed cowering in my room and peeked out the windows like a disgruntled child. My chest tightened when I saw Adam strolling about with a group enjoying the gardens.

His lovemaking had left me shaken. More than ever I felt fragmented as warring feelings pulled me in all directions. I wondered how soon Adam would make his move. I didn't know where in the house the family jewels were kept but I was pretty certain that Adam had already located the safe. Maybe he would be there when the black velvet trays were brought out. He might be planning to steal them before the party, I thought. I closed my eyes and pressed my forehead against the window frame, trying to blot out the scene that would follow. How would I be able to pretend ignorance when people like Pamela leveled an accusing finger at me? Would I be branded as an accomplice? Who would believe the weird story of a hostage bride?

A knock at the bedroom door startled me. As I crossed the room to open the door, I tried to compose myself, making certain the buttons on my day dress were fastened to the high lace collar. I knew it wasn't Adam—or a servant.

It was Professor Lynwood. He wore a baggy pair of trousers and a loose jacket as if he'd been bicycling. "Charlotte, my dear, they told me you weren't feeling well," he said with his unruly bushy eyebrows matted in a concerned frown.

"Just a headache. Please come in." I led him

into the small sitting room and we sat down on the settee together.

"I brought you something to while away the time," he said, handing me an old leather-bound photograph album. "Reminiscences of my Oxford days. You'll find many photographs of your father in there. And several of your mother, too. She was such a pretty thing, she was. Might have married her myself given half a chance. And then you would have been my daughter." He said it with such wistfulness that I impulsively hugged him.

The affectionate gesture brought a warm glow to his face. "You've made me realize how much I've missed." Then he cleared his throat. "Anyway, I thought you might like taking a jaunt through the past with me."

A deep loneliness came through his words and manner. He had been a man dedicated to his work and the ridicule he had received when his United States invention failed had caused him to abandon the project. It must have been terribly hard on him to come home as a failure, I thought sadly. I knew there was bitterness there. I remembered hearing my father say that our government had been too hard on him. I was glad that I could do my little bit to dull that hurt.

For nearly an hour, we sat side by side and looked through the album together. He had a story for almost every picture and in the faded photographs I saw my father as a young man.

The same cheery smile had remained with him through the years and my eyes misted with homesickness as a youthful father looked back at me. Then the Professor pointed out a pretty young girl looking at the camera with wide eyes that matched my own. I gazed at my mother who had died in an influenza epidemic when I was a baby. "You look a lot like her . . . act like her, too. I'm glad you came to Lynwood, Charlotte. It's meant a lot to me."

I swallowed. I hoped he would feel the same way after my husband betrayed us both. "Thank you. I'll tell my father how kind you've been."

"Keep the album. I want you to have it. Take it back and show it to your father. I want him to know how much I admire you, Charlotte . . . and what this visit has meant to me. He's a very rich man, you know . . . having a daughter like you."

I smiled at that for our little house would nearly fit in his spacious family parlor and our furniture was serviceable and unpretentious.

"There are many kinds of riches," he said as if reading my thoughts. "Life has a way of balancing out our rewards, doesn't it. I have Lynwood Manor, an extensive family inheritance and international recognition in my field—and he has you. The balance is in his favor. Take good care of him, my dear."

"Yes, I will." The Professor would understand why I couldn't put my father in jeopardy. Why I had to go along with the scheme to rob him. When it all came out, he would understand my loyalty. I held the album tenderly in my hands. "We will treasure this gift," I said in a husky voice.

He leaned over and kissed my cheek. "Well, I must get downstairs. Pamela will never forgive me if I don't act the gracious host. I never did care for this kind of folderol but Pamela and Larry have borne the responsibility for Lynwood Manor all the years I've been shuttling back and forth to America."

"They love you very much," I said and was surprised to see a shadow flutter across his face.

"I wonder?" he said quietly and then shook himself. "Well, now. When you're feeling better come downstairs and help me endure the polite fripperies of Pamela's pleasure-seeking crowd."

After he had gone, I felt my usual resilience surging back. Why was I cowering here in my room? It wasn't my nature. My father had always chided me for charging into situations with the confidence of Hannibal crossing the Alps. I should be using my wits to thwart any foul deed my husband-thief was preparing to execute. Somehow, without sacrificing my father's welfare, I had to stop him. Yes, I would stay at Adam's side, watch his every move and keep him from carrying out the theft of the jewels.

I put on a pretty green gown with a floral overlay skirt that we had bought in London. Brushing my hair into a mass of auburn curls, I fastened them at the nape of my neck instead of in my usual chignon. Impulsively I stuck a small rose over one ear. My appearance gave me courage. I knew that he was trapped by the same physical attraction that held me captive in his arms. I was not above using it to my advantage if given the chance.

He was obviously amused by my sudden arrival at his side and my display of wifely devotion. I gave all my attention to him like a bride who couldn't bear to be inches away from his side. We moved through the formal rooms as a couple and when we finally went upstairs to dress for dinner, I was more confident than ever that I wasn't going to let him out of my sight the entire evening.

"Careful," he teased me as we dressed for the formal dinner which would precede the ball. "Your behavior is most suspect."

"What do you mean?" I pretended innocence.

"You're sticking to me like a cocklebur on a horse's tail."

"Well, you got the right end of the resemblance!" I quipped.

He threw back his head and laughed. "You never cease to surprise me, darling. Who would have thought you capable of such bawdy wit?"

"I'm capable of a lot more things that you might suspect," I countered, foolishly confident that I was capable of matching wits with him.

"You think I'm going to steal those jewels tonight, don't you?"

"Aren't you?"

"Of course not." His lips quirked in a teasing

smile. Was he laughing at me or at the idea that he was a jewel thief?

"That's why we're here, isn't it? You can't wait to get your greedy hands on a fortune." Suddenly I couldn't keep up the banter . . . the pretense. "Let's leave now. We can hire a coach . . . go back to London . . . back to the house on Regency Street. I'm afraid of what's going to happen. Please, Adam . . . don't do this." I looked pleadingly up into his face.

He took me in his arms then, quietly and gently. There was no anger like the last time. His fingertips traced the smooth curve of my cheek and then he slowly bent his head, putting his mouth on mine. His kiss was soft, as if tinged with regret. He kissed my eyelids and then playfully rubbed his nose against mine. He threaded a curl on my forehead with his finger. "I love you, Charl," he murmured.

"Then you'll go? You'll give up this insanity—?"

"I can't."

"You mean you *won't*."

"I mean I *can't*."

"Why not?" I flared. "You never hesitate to do what you want any other time. If you want to leave now, you can. We can pack and be gone before dinner."

"Charl, you don't understand what's involved—"

"How can I—when you won't tell me?"

"I don't want to endanger you. I'm thinking of your safety. If you don't know anything, you'll

241

be safe."

"Safe from what? Don't you see . . . whatever happens, I'll be accused of being your accomplice. How is that going to keep me safe? I might even go to prison—"

"Don't be melodramatic, Charl!" His voice had lost its softness and was ribbed with cold command. "Just enjoy yourself tonight and quit trying to second-guess me. You're out of your depth!"

"We'll see about that!" I flung myself out of his arms and finished dressing in stony silence. My evening gown was one which Adam had bought for me in London . . . to make up for the wedding gown I had missed, he had said. At the time, I had thought it beautiful but I wore it tonight without joy, selecting it only because nothing else in my wardrobe was suitable for the gala affair. The gown was pearl-white and fashioned of satin brocade with an overskirt of chiffon. Pale lavender silk flowers were caught in flounces across the front and in the back, rows of chiffon ruffles fell to the floor in a slight train. My shoulders were bare and long white gloves were embroidered in the same pale shades of lavender as the silk flowers of the gown. I swept my hair up in a coronet of auburn curls and placed a small jeweled feather amidst the curls. My appearance startled me. There was no sign of inner turmoil in the fashionably dressed young woman reflected in my vanity mirror, exuding sophistication and even beauty. I had to remind myself that it was really me reflected in the silvered glass.

As always, Adam wore evening attire with an air of graceful masculinity that eluded most men in stiff collars and ruffled shirts. He wore a tapering black coat with formal tails which smoothly fitted his broad shoulders an narrow waist. Narrow trousers molded his long, firm legs and I was taunted by the memory of those limbs pressed against mine. I had once called Adam the devil—and I knew it must be true. No matter how evil he seemed to be, I couldn't stop loving him.

When we came down the elegant stairway, Larry's eyes widened as he saw me. I was rather amused. He seemed ill at ease as if I had suddenly turned into a stranger. He stammered a stream of compliments then scooted away, his round face flushed from the encounter.

Adam gave a quiet chuckle. "I told you that you'd made a conquest." He obviously was amused at Larry's love-struck behavior but when Freddy turned his appraising eyes upon me amusement faded in Adam's face. His eyes turned to wintry, icy gray.

As much to spite Adam as anything, I smiled coquettishly at Freddy. I suddenly felt the surge of power that every woman feels when a handsome man looks at her the way Freddy was looking at me. His eyes deliberately traveled over the tight bodice and lingered on my full breasts thrusting above the lace edge of my gown. "Exquisite," he murmured in bold appraisal. When he kissed my hand, I couldn't hide the color rising in my cheeks.

I looked beyond him and saw that Pamela was standing only a few steps away. She had watched the encounter and her dark eyes smoldered. Moving with the stiff, straight carriage of a royal personage, she swept over to us. She had chosen black velvet which showed off her white skin and made a beautiful background for the array of diamonds and rubies hanging around her neck and dangling from her ears.

The jewels! My heart raced as Adam moved forward to greet her.

He gave her his rare smile. " 'She walks in beauty like the night.' I'm sure the poet must have had you in mind, Pamela, when he penned those words. You look lovely."

For a moment a flicker of a smile softened the hard lines of her mouth. "Thank you."

"That necklace is absolutely beyond belief," Adam said, staring at it.

"A hundred perfect stones," she said, touching the mesh of diamonds, rubies and gold which she wore like a queen's collar. The stones radiated blinding prisms of color. I knew now why Adam had sacrificed my cousin's emeralds. "My great-grandfather brought the gems from all over the world and had the jewels set in this necklace."

"Exquisite," murmured Adam.

In a warning gesture, I slipped my arm through Adam's. "Yes, the necklace is magnificent," I said, smiling at Pamela. "I've never seen anything so beautiful . . . you must be a little uneasy about wearing it, Pamela."

Her dark eyes coldly met mine and her long neck seemed to visibly lengthen. "Jewelry is to be worn, is it not?"

I had no answer but a polite one. "Yes, of course." I wondered if this audacious display of wealth was intended to sway Freddy into proposing.

The evening took on a nightmarish quality. I said the right things, made the correct responses but the center of my consciousness was removed from delivering the proper social amenities.

Dinner was served in an opulent banquet hall which I had not seen before. Its ceiling was an elaborate network of arches, lofty and beautifully decorated with hand-painted idyllic scenes of shepherds and shepherdesses . . . looking more French than English, I thought. Huge Flemish tapestries graced the walls, framed by a wide, sculptured molding which ran the length of the dining hall. Professor Lynwood had said his ancestors had made their fortune in commerce. There was evidence everywhere that it had been a propserous venture, I thought wryly, musing about the English class system which looked down on this kind of wealth.

The long table shimmered with crystal, silver and delicate oyster-white porcelain. Pamela took her place at one end and the Professor at the other. They sat in high-backed throne chairs

which matched smaller ones flanking the table.
There were no place cards and I was grateful
when Professor Lynwood politely motioned us
to his end of the table. Freddy was seated on one
side of Pamela and Larry on the other. The rest
of the guests found seats in an unobtrusive
manner and a quiet murmuring of voices began
as a procession of servants entered through a
wide paneled door at one end of the hall.

I must have shown some bewilderment at the
array of silverware as I placed a white damask
napkin in my lap, because Adam whispered
reassuringly that I should just proceed from the
outside utensil inward as various dishes were
presented. Later I couldn't remember everything I'd eaten for the parade of aromatic food
went on for almost three hours. When we
finally reached the last course, I wondered if
my gown would burst its seams when I stood up
again.

"How does that compare with my cooking?"
asked Adam as we made our way upstairs to the
second floor ballroom. The question brought
back the poignant intimacy we had shared in
the London house. He had always prepared
breakfast, often bringing it to me in bed as I lay
satiated with love in the rumpled bedclothes.
Why couldn't life always be like that? Why did
he have to destroy everything? My lips must
have quivered for he whispered, "Oh ye of little
faith."

"What does that mean?"

"Simply that you should enjoy yourself

tonight . . . and quit looking at me as if I've slipped some of the silver into my pocket."

"Have you?"

"Of course not," he grinned. "And I'm not going to take the jewels off Pamela's neck, either."

Did that mean he planned to snatch them later, after everyone had retired? I didn't have a chance to voice this apprehension. We were ushered to one end of the ballroom and seated on white gilded chairs. Pamela had arranged for a brief musical recital to take place after dinner. Undoubtedly, the interlude was designed to give her guests time to digest their meal before the small orchestra in the gallery called them to the dance floor.

I could not keep my mind on the offerings of the flutist and pianist, although I'm certain that Chopin and Debussy had never been rendered more beautifully. A woman next to me whispered that the musicians had been brought from London for the occasion.

Pamela had certainly not spared any expense. I sent a few furtive looks in her direction, wondering why she had set her sights on a man she met aboard ship. Surely, that was no guarantee of a lasting relationship. Then I chided myself for the hypocrite that I was. Holding my hands tightly in my lap, I knew that I was in no position to judge anyone about affairs of the heart.

I was glad when the musicale was over and the ball began. With the same kind of mesmerizing attraction that had been there when we danced aboard the Lucania, Adam made me forget everything else but the joy of being in his arms. He seemed relaxed and content to enjoy himself. In spite of myself, tension eased out of my body and I was lulled into a false sense of security.

When Larry asked me to dance, the impulse to refuse was very great. I didn't want to let Adam out of my sight . . . not even for the space of one dance. Yet, I couldn't hurt Larry's feelings.

"I should dance with our hostess," Adam said with maddening understanding of my hesitation. I knew he was laughing at me but nonetheless I was glad to have him within sight while Larry guided me not too gracefully around the floor.

"It's a lovely party," I said, trying to make conversation. Larry was still looking at me as if I were some fragile creature that demanded careful and formal behavior.

He nodded. His blue eyes refused to meet mine.

"How's the mare doing? The one you showed me the other day—"

His head came up. His expression brightened. "She foaled this afternoon—pretty little filly."

"How wonderful? Is she a sorrel?"

"No, dark bay, like the stud. Has the same strong withers, too." He suddenly became a better dancer as he forgot where he was and chatted excitedly about his new addition to the stables.

I encouraged him with a smile and a nod while keeping one eye on Adam and Pamela as they moved together around the floor. When the dance was over, we started back to the place where Adam and I had been sitting but were stopped in the middle of the floor by Freddy who winked lasciviously at me.

"I've been waiting for your possessive husband to turn you loose so I could claim a dance. Thank you, Larry, for whisking her away. Now it's my turn." Freddy bowed gallantly. "If you would honor me with the next dance."

Larry glared at Freddy but turned away and left us standing together at the edge of the dance floor.

I shot a glance at Adam and saw that he was still with Pamela. They stood near the refreshment table and I saw a glass of champagne in each of their hands.

"It's all right," laughed Freddy. "A wife doesn't have to be at her husband's side *every* minute. And you have nothing to fear from Pamela. She's definitely not Adam's type."

"Is she yours?" I asked boldly.

"Every lovely woman is my type," he grinned.

"It's quite obvious that you are the one who has captured her heart," I said with shameful boldness. He shrugged and I suddenly wanted to plead with him not to hurt her. The impulse was foolish. Pamela had never liked me and would fiercely resent my interference. I remembered the scene between him and Larry aboard ship. I was certain Larry had been warning him not to hurt his sister.

"Pamela's a very remarkable lady," he said smoothly as we danced. "But she lacks the fiery beauty of a certain lady I know. When I first saw you aboard ship, I felt a deep stab of regret. Ah, what a bittersweet fate that we met too late." He sighed heavily.

His languid expression only made me laugh. I knew that he was the kind of man to be intrigued by that which he could not have. If he married Pamela, he would never be satisfied with her or what she could bring him. He would always want more. Even now, as he was flattering me, I had the feeling he was considering other conquests dancing by us who might be more interesting.

I was glad when the music ended and he took me back to Adam. Pamela had disappeared and Adam was talking to Professor Lynwood.

"Do you think you could suffer an old man's halting steps for one slow dance, my dear Charlotte?" the Professor asked as I joined them.

"Of course. I would be delighted." He had seemed slightly pensive most of the evening and even at dinner I had failed to change his mood. I had the feeling that he would prefer a smelly old laboratory to this rose-perfumed, mirrored ballroom. I wondered if he had ever really enjoyed this magnificent ballroom even in his youth. None of the photographs showed him with a girl. Even when he was a student at Oxford with my father, he must have been too studious and serious to have much of a social life.

He was not a natural dancer and his movements were quite mechanical but I enjoyed myself. He was such good company and was quite sprightly as he guided me through the steps. When the music stopped we were in front of a terrace door and before I could gracefully decline, he led me outside to stand at a railing overlooking the gardens. He smiled at me and seemed to be enjoying himself. I knew that I couldn't abruptly excuse myself and leave him here.

"Beautiful view from here, isn't it? You can even see the moonlight shining on the water. And listen—hear the sound of the surf upon the rocks. Gets mighty fierce sometimes."

"Yes, it has a melancholy sound, doesn't it? As if it's searching for something it can't find," I said, listening to the relentless rise and fall of the water. "I guess I prefer the quiet Delaware River," I confessed. "My father and I love to go down to the wharf and watch the ships."

"You miss him, don't you?"

"Yes."

"When do you think you'll be heading back? Or are you going to extend your honeymoon and tour the continent?"

His questions brought back a rush of anxiety.

"I want to go home soon."

He nodded. "And where will you and Adam live?"

"I don't know . . . our plans are indefinite." The question reminded me that I had tarried too long out of Adam's sight. "Shall we go back in now, Professor? I think my husband might be looking for me."

"Of course. You shouldn't let an old man monopolize you."

"It isn't that. I'd love to stay here with you . . . but . . . but I think I'd better go in," I stammered. I had lost track of Adam while I danced with the Professor and a growing anxiety made me search the milling crowd as we made our way back inside.

I didn't see him anywhere.

"I believe I'll call it a night," said the Professor. "Slip back into my study and let you young people carry on."

"Thank you for the dance . . . and conversation."

"My pleasure."

I thought he looked tired and somewhat preoccupied as he made his way downstairs. Once more, I scanned the crowded ballroom looking for Adam. Then I went out of the room and looked over the railing at the broad hall below. A few guests had collected in groups, talking and laughing and toasting each other with champagne—but Adam was not among them.

Where had he gone?

I lifted my skirts and went downstairs. As

discreetly as possible I searched the front of the house, passing quickly through the elegant salon, banquet room and wide halls. Several times I was forced to stop and speak to people but I detached myself as quickly as I could and hurried down the wide corridor which led to the south wing where the family lived. The half-opened door of the Professor's study caught my eye. I could see a light shining through the crack.

I gave a polite knock, thinking I would ask the Professor if he had seen Adam. No one answered. I pushed the door open and stepped inside.

At first I only noted that the chair behind the Professor's large English-style desk was empty but as my gaze swung away, I saw him lying prone on the floor, half-hidden behind the desk.

I screamed and lurched forward. Throwing myself down beside him, I lifted his head. The Professor's eyes were rolled back in his skull with only the whites showing. There were papers all over the floor spattered with the blood spewing from a wound on his head.

He must have intruded on someone going through his papers! The knowledge was like blinders suddenly jerked from my eyes and the realization was like a shot of pain.

I knew then it was *not* jewels that Adam had come to steal!

14

Winston, the butler, answered my frantic bell.

"The Professor's been hurt. Get a doctor!"

I didn't know his pudgy frame could move so fast. He quickly located a doctor among the guests and returned with Dr. Benedict, a tall, emaciated-looking man who looked as though the weight of illness and death through the years had taken their toll.

I stuffed my fists into my mouth as I watched him examine the prone body. Then he stood up and told Winston to get a couple of servants to carry the injured man up to bed. It was done with such efficiency that I don't think anyone partying at the front of the house was aware that the assault had taken place.

I waited outside the Professor's bedroom door to hear the extent of his injuries. I was sure that he was dying. Murder! The ugly word terrified me. The strains of music and peals of laughter floating into this wing from the front of the house was a mockery to the drama going on in the Professor's bedroom.

At last the doctor came out into the hall.

"Is he—?"

The older gentleman read the unspoken word on my white lips. "Dead?" He shook his white head. "No. But critical." Then he told me that Professor Lynwood had suffered a severe concussion. "He must have fallen and hit his head. Probably too much champagne."

I knew it wasn't true. I had been with him when he excused himself to go down to his study. He had not been drinking heavily. No, the Professor had not fallen. I was convinced he had returned to his study and discovered someone going through his papers. I wondered if he had seen them or if he had been struck from behind. If he could identify the assailant when he regained consciousness, I feared that name that would be on his lips and put him in more danger.

Doctor Benedict summoned Larry and Pamela into the family parlor to tell them what had happened. Adam and Freddy came with them.

"What happened?" Adam came to my side where I sat in a chair still in my blood-stained dress.

"I could not raise my eyes to look at him.

"Are you hurt?"

I wanted to laugh hysterically. He was a consummate actor! The look I gave him made him stiffen. *Yes, I know.* The unspoken message was like a sword raised between us. I looked at the jewels around Pamela's neck and then back at Adam. I wanted to pound my fists against his chest but I just sat there and listened as the doctor reported the seriousness of the Professor's wound.

"Concussion . . . if he regains consciousness within twenty-four hours, he'll probably make it. If not—" He shrugged.

Pamela wept and turned to Freddy's shoulder for comfort. "Poor Uncle . . . my party . . . my wonderful party . . . ruined."

"He's not going to die, is he?" Larry stammered. He looked like a frightened small boy. "I couldn't handle all of this by myself. It's too much responsibility—I don't have a good head for business. I've tried but—" He bit his lip.

"We must hope for the best," was the only comfort the Doctor offered.

I fled from the room then. Sobbing, I ran down the corridor to our room and flung myself on the bed. It was worse than even I had imagined. And it was my fault. I should have done something—told the Professor, warned him that we were not what we seemed.

Adam came in then. I stiffened as Adam sat down on the edge of the bed. "Go away!" I sobbed.

He turned me over, putting his hands on each side of my face so that I was forced to look at him. "Charl . . . darling . . . I didn't want this to happen—"

The tears dried on my cheeks. I suddenly felt cold and numb. "What were you looking for?" My question was a sharp knife slicing the thick air between us. "You didn't come here for Pamela's jewels, did you?"

"No," he sighed. "I told you that all along. You were the one who had me identified as a jewel thief!"

"You lied to me—"

"I just let you think what you wanted to think. It was safer that way."

"To let me think you were going to rob the Lynwoods?"

"Yes." He sat down and rested his head in his hands.

"What is it?" I choked. "Why did you bring me here? What do you want? You have to tell me now. I can't take any more." My voice rose hysterically. "The Professor struck down."

"I didn't do it, Charl. I know you don't believe me but—"

"Jasper!" My eyes widened. "He must have been searching the Professor's papers while you stayed in view at the party."

"No, he didn't do it."

"Then you must have. You left while I was dancing with the Professor—you thought it was safe to ransack his papers—but the Professor came in unexpectedly. You hit him—maybe killed him!"

"Stop it!" He grabbed my hands. "Please, Charl. Don't look at me like that—"

"You say you love me," I sobbed.

"I do! And that's what makes it so hard. I never intended that my feelings would get tangled like this." His hands were ice-cold in mine.

"Then tell me the truth . . . all of it . . . please—"

The gray in his eyes intensified and he studied me as if weighing the consequences.

"Please—" I begged.

He raised my hands and kissed them gently, a pained look crossing his face. "I'll never forgive myself if I bring you to harm." He sighed heavily and then began to speak. "I thought it best that you didn't know . . . safer for you. But now—" He took a deep breath. "As you know Professor Lynwood has been trying for nearly ten years to put an aeroplane in the air. The U.S. government paid him considerable money to come to the United States and conduct his experiments. His last efforts were very promising but ended in failure. He was accused of wasting the money the government had given him. The public ridicule made him decide to come back to England. Word got out that he was leaving the country with *new* plans."

"New plans?"

"Yes. He solved the problem which caused

the failure but he was so angry that he decided to keep the correction a secret. He had drawings which corrected the defect that had kept his man-size aerodome from launching. Instead of turning them over to the U.S. government, the Professor left the country with the new blueprints. These new plans are worth millions to any nation endeavoring to put a flying machine into the air. On the world black market, anyone with these new drawings could command his price."

I was sick to my stomach. In some ways I wished that it was jewels that Adam had been after. His cold, calculated plan to steal the Professor's invention was even more detestable. It was worth millions. No wonder he laughed at my mistaken belief that he was after a handful of jewels. "And you used me to get close to him! So that you could steal the plans."

He nodded. "I needed access to his house . . . to his study. I wanted to get my hands on that revised document."

"But why didn't we come here directly . . . instead of spending time in London?"

"Because I wasn't certain that the plans hadn't already been sold to a foreign power . . . like Germany."

"He wouldn't do that!"

"He was angry enough to do exactly that! Not for money—but for revenge."

"And you wanted to steal them and sell them yourself?"

His mouth tightened. "What else? Why would I risk my neck if not for money?" he answered sarcastically.

"But you didn't find them."

"No. But apparently someone else is looking for them too."

"How do I know that you aren't just making all of this up? Why should I believe that it wasn't you or Jasper who struck down the Professor?"

"You don't . . . unless you accept my word for it."

"How can I? You deliberately dragged me into this mesh of deceit and greed! And Cousin Della—what really happened to her?"

"She's in jail."

I blinked as if my confused mine would not handle the information.

"Jail?"

He nodded. "I made sure the police learned about her smuggling activities. I came to the house and advised her that she was going to be arrested—"

"That's when she wrote the note."

"Yes, she pulled a fast one on me by going into her study with the pretense that she wanted to leave a note for the cleaning woman . . . but the police arrived almost at the same time and I thought she hadn't had time to write anything. I didn't know she'd crammed a half-finished note into a cubbyhole of her desk."

"And my father?"

"He's being looked after," he said shortly.

I knew then that the nightmare was not over. Now that I knew what the deception was all about, the nefarious scheme was even more treacherous. Adam wanted those revised drawings. He was going to insure my cooperation until he found them.

I got up and walked over to the window, pulled back the curtain and stared out into the night. A lovely, serene patina of golden moonlight upon the gardens and the sea was a mockery to the stark despair within me. If I had ever doubted that my father was in real danger, that doubt was gone. Adam was not in this thing alone. The stakes were too high for Adam and his fellow conspirators to release me from my hostage status. No wonder he had not wanted me to know the truth. He had been glad that my attention had been centered on Pamela's jewels. How he must have laughed at my feeble efforts to prevent him from being alone with her.

I blinked against a hot fullness in my eyes. I did not know what I could do. Knowing the real reason for the charade only seemed to involve me even more in it.

"I'm sorry, Charl," he said quietly, coming up behind me and resting his hands on my shoulders.

"About what? That you failed tonight? Or about your betrayal?"

"All of that . . . and more, I guess." His voice was wintry as he said, "I have to find the revised blueprints."

I knew then that I couldn't let it happen. I did not believe it had been someone else who had attacked Professor Lynwood. I had seen the fierce, cold determination in Adam's eyes. Nothing would stop him from trying to get the corrections for the Professor's invention. From the beginning he had carried out every detail of the deceit with brutal cunning. And he had been correct in his decision not to tell me the truth. Now my determination to thwart him was even greater than when I thought him a jewel thief. Somehow I had to convince him that he had neutralized me by telling me the truth. Make him think that I would not interfere.

He pulled me gently back against him. His lips touched my hairline. I stiffened against his touch. Some involuntary part of me wanted to relax and feel the sweet length of his body against mine. It was no pretense when warmth eased away the deep bittersweet pain that churned within me. It took all the self-discipline I could summon to withdraw from his arms.

"It's late," I murmured. "I'm too tired to think clearly." I went into the spacious dressing room and closed the door. I leaned up against it, pressing my hands against the panels, choking back a cry of anguish that leaped into my throat.

When I came out, he had gone. I went to the door of the sitting room and looked in. He was already stretched out on the small daybed. "What is it, Charl? Did you want something?" he asked without taking his gaze off the ceiling.

There was a weary edge to his voice that twisted my heart before I could dismiss it.

"No . . . I was just making sure—"

"That I was still here?"

"Yes."

"Stay out of this, Charl. Don't be foolish enough to try and interfere."

I turned away and this time the tears streaming down my cheeks were hot and angry. I clenched my fists until my nails bit cruelly into my flesh . . . and I didn't even feel the pain.

Professor Lynwood's condition had not changed the next morning. Breakfast was a silent affair in the family dining room. Everyone was tired and short-tempered. Freddy and Pamela snapped at each other like an old married couple. I decided his stay as a house guest was about over . . . unless he had decided to propose to Pamela after all. Larry excused himself quickly, murmuring something about being needed in the stables and Adam volunteered to go with him.

Even the servants seemed less efficient; they were tired in the aftermath of the party. After listlessly poking at my breakfast, I made my way to the Professor's room. The door was open. A nurse sat by his bed and stood up like a guard dog when I came in.

"How is he?" I whispered, looking down at the Professor's still form. His weathered face, flaccid skin and relaxed facial muscles showed his sixty years. A liver-spotted hand lay outside the covers and I touched it affectionately. Blinking back tears, I sat down in a nearby chair.

"If you are going to be here a few minutes," the matronly nurse said, "I'll slip out for a breath of air. Doctor called me in the middle of the night . . . and I haven't had any breakfast yet."

"Of course. Take your time."

She left and I was glad to just sit by his bed. I was weary from a sleepless night and thoughts too heavy to be put aside. If only I could talk with him . . . sort out my confused thoughts. I took his hand again and squeezed it, hoping to feel some responding tension. "Please, wake up . . . there are so many things we need to talk about. I don't know what I should do." My voice cracked.

His hand remained cold and flaccid.

I bowed my head and let the tears come. I was so engrossed in my own self-pity that for a moment I didn't hear the soft strangled whisper, "Charlotte—"

My head jerked up and I brushed away my tears. "Yes . . . yes . . . I'm here." I bent over his bed and looked into his half-closed eyes. "You're awake . . . Thank God, you're awake—"

"Charlotte—"

"Yes, it's me. I'm right here."

"Your father—" he croaked.

"No, he's not here. Just me, Charlotte . . .

don't you remember?'' His mind must be befuddled from the blow. His memory was distorted.

"The album—''

"Yes, you showed me the album—''

"Your father—''

"I'll give the album to my father," I reassured him. "I'll take it home. But you have to get well . . . I need to talk to you.''

"Picture . . . your mother—''

"Yes, I remember . . . the picture of my mother . . . I'll give it to him.''

Why was his mind centered on the album? Maybe he didn't want to give the picture of my mother away. Suddenly I knew that he had never married because the woman he wanted had married someone else. He had been in love with my mother. And he loved me for the daughter he had never had. I bent over and kissed his cheek. "Please, get well," I pleaded in a choked voice. "I love you very much.''

I thought there was a slight quiver at the corner of his lips, like a faint smile. He closed his eyes again but his breathing seemed stronger. He was going to get well. I knew it. Thank God. Thank God!

When the nurse came back, I told her that the Professor had regained consciousness.

"Then he's going to make it," she said with positive authority as if a patient had never proved her wrong.

I went back to my room and felt giddy with

relief. As soon as I could talk to the Professor, I would tell him about Adam's plan to steal his new blueprints. He would know what to do. I was certain that Professor Lynwood would protect me. In order to keep my father safe, Adam must not know that I had betrayed him. And what would happen after the drawings were beyond Adam's reach, I did not know. I could not think that far ahead. My own emotions were too tangled to be sorted out rationally.

I must make certain that I took the album to my father . . . but I decided I wanted to leave the picture of my mother with the Professor. It was on his mind and he obviously had changed his mind about giving it away.

I slipped the fading brown photograph out of its four cornered tabs. It felt rather thick in my hands. Curious, I turned it and discovered a folded piece of paper taped to the back.

A love letter to my mother, hiding behind her picture and perhaps forgotten? I knew I shouldn't open it but I couldn't help myself. No, it wasn't a letter . . . I suddenly felt as if someone had punched me in the stomach. It was a detailed drawing. The Professor had hidden it there.

The blueprint didn't mean anything to me but I knew what it was.

The detailed correction of Professor Lynwood's flying machine.

I sat there staring at it. He had tried to tell me

it was there. No wonder that picture had been on his mind. He was afraid he was going to die before he had alerted my father that it was there. *He wanted to send it back to the United States.*

I carefully refolded the paper and attached it to the back of my mother's picture again, putting it back in the album. That piece of paper was worth millions to any country hoping to master the power of flight. And I had it! Hysterical laughter erupted from my throat and I put a fist up to muffle the sound. The charade was over! I had beaten Adam Demorest.

As if in response to my gleeful thoughts, he loomed up in the doorway, taking me by surprise. I removed my hand from my mouth and swallowed back the laughter in my throat. His quizzical expression made me stammer, "I . . . I thought you were at the stables with Larry."

"We decided to cut our ride short and come back. Looks like rain. Larry's worried about his uncle. He's with him now. What are you doing with the album?"

"Just looking at it," I answered, trying to compose myself. "I was homesick . . . for my father."

"How's the Professor?"

"The same," I lied. He mustn't know the Professor had regained consciousness and spoken to me. If I repeated what he had said,

Adam would know immediately that the photograph album was important.

I stood up as casually as I could. "I feel like a little walk in the garden before lunch to get a breath of fresh air."

His eyes went from my face to the old book I clutched in my hands.

"Where'd you get the album?" he asked casually. Too casually, I thought.

"The professor. He gave it to me several days ago."

His penetrating gaze fixed on my face. I knew then I should casually toss it aside as if it were of no importance—but I couldn't. The precious secret it contained governed my decision not to let it out of my sight.

"What's in it?"

"Pictures of the Professor and my father when they were at Oxford."

I brushed past him. He knew me too well. I knew my behavior was making him suspicious but there was nothing I could do about it. With the album clutched in my hand I hurried down the family staircase.

Just as I reached the bottom, Pamela came out of her uncle's study with Freddy. They were quarreling and their voices carried down the hall.

"I'll thank you to pack your things and leave!" she snapped.

"For all your breeding, you're something of a bitch, Pamela!"

"And you're nothing but a fortune hunter!"

"Not true . . . and that's what galls you, isn't it? Flaunting all your uncle's wealth in front of me hasn't bought you a husband."

"I wouldn't marry you if—"

"If I were the last man on earth!" he finished with a cruel laugh. "If you were the last woman around you'd never get a husband. You're so starchy, a man gets scratched just looking at you."

There was no chance to make a hasty retreat back up the stairs before they reached me. I know my face betrayed my involuntary eavesdropping. "Good morning," I stammered.

"Good morning," responded Freddy, his expression changing. The furrows on his forehead smoothing out. "It's a welcome change to see your lovely face this morning."

"Isn't that my uncle's album?" demanded Pamela, her eyes fixing on the old leather-bound book.

"Yes . . . Professor Lynwood gave it to me," I said quickly, "—to take back to my father."

"He'd never do that!" snapped Pamela. "He's always mooning over some woman's picture in it!"

"He gave it to me. When he gets well you can ask him," I countered, new anxiety building that she might demand the album from me. "I'm not lying, Pamela."

She elevated her long neck. "I'm only suggesting that my uncle would not give that album . . . to anyone."

"Now, Pamela, don't be so greedy," chided Freddy. "Your uncle has the right to give away his things if he wants to. Why should you care about an old faded photograph album?"

"It's up to me and Larry to see that people don't take advantage of him!" Her black eyes were accusing. "Just how long do you and your husband plan to take advantage of his hospitality, Charlotte?"

"*I* expect to be leaving Lynwood Hall very soon." My answer was as cool as her question.

"That makes two of us," said Freddy. "What about Adam? Is he going with you?" He looked at me with a questioning smile.

I flushed. Could it be that Freddy knew about our less than blissful sleeping arrangements? "Of course," I said with as much indignation as I could manage. "Now, if you'll excuse me—" Without looking at either of them, I walked on down the hall and out a terrace door.

I was outside before I dared let out my breath. My heart raced and thumped loudly in my ears. I didn't know what I would have done if Pamela had demanded her uncle's album back. It would be foolish to carry the album everywhere. My behavior had destroyed it as an inconspicuous hiding place. I would have to remove the blueprint and hide it on my person.

The day was gray and overcast. A weighted stillness filled the air. Insects that usually kept the garden humming with summer noises had already fled the approaching storm. I could see a dark bank of rain clouds masking the horizon like an enveloping shroud. Even though the storm was still far out to sea, ruffled waters rose and fell in greater swells as the wind swept over them. The rising surf pounded and lashed against the cliff. Ordinarily I would have turned back to the house but the immense secret I clutched in my hands drove me down a narrow garden path caught between precisely trimmed evergreen hedges until I found a garden bench which was set under a rounded trellis covered by a mass of trailing roses.

I sat down and searched the garden path in both directions. It was empty but I couldn't see over the high, maze-like hedges to ascertain if anyone lurked there. The garden, usually so alive with color, was misted and blurred with moisture-laden air, like the too-wet strokes of an artist's brush upon a garden scene. I caught my breath for my heart was racing as I tried to reassure myself that I was alone.

Then I opened the album and took out the photograph of my mother. Her wide eyes smiled at me as if reinforcing my belief that two men had been in love with her. I wondered if she had ever felt about my father the way I felt about Adam. The capacity for such loving and bewildering passion must have been inherited, I thought. She must have been . . . The thought was never completed.

A sixth sense brought my head up—too late! A blow from behind pitched me forward and sent me sprawling on the ground.

For several minutes, I fought drifting black

swirls of unconsciousness. My heavy head flopped grotesquely on my weak neck as I tried to raise myself. Finally, with great force of will, I struggled to my knees.

The album lay on the ground nearby and the picture and paper I had been holding in my hand were gone.

Someone had followed me into the garden and taken them!

15

A heavy rumbling like approaching cannon fire accompanied the disappearance of the sun behind angry dark clouds. My hair whipped free of its pinnings. I did not know what to do. My thoughts refused to clear. Like the tree branches suddenly whipping around me, I could not put them into any neat, rational pattern. Only one fact remained clear. Someone had taken the precious drawing which the Professor had hidden in the album.

I stumbled forward, my frantic eyes searching for the figure who had struck me and fled. Adam? Had he followed me out into the garden, watched me open the book and remove the paper from behind my mother's picture? Should I go back to the house? Tell someone? Who?

The surface of the sea was black now, reflecting the black canopy overhead. Above the relentless pounding of a rising surf upon sullen rock, I heard a horse's neigh. The sound drew me in the direction of the stables. When I reached it, I hung back in the shadows and saw Adam standing in the stable doorway looking around. At that moment, Jasper hurried forward from the same side of the garden where I had been sitting! His thin face was alive with excitement. He drew Adam back into the shadows of the barn and I could only see a vague movement of arms as the two conspirators talked together.

I did not need to hear them to guess what was happening. Jasper was turning over the valuable piece of paper. He must have been in the garden when I sat down . . . and had circled behind me. What a fool I'd been. I had played right into their hands.

All fight went out of me as I stumbled away. Heartsick and defeated, I wanted to crawl into some protective burrow like a wounded animal and hide from the world. If I raised a hue and cry about the stolen document, I could put my father in danger. There was nothing I could do. Now that Adam had secured what he wanted, he would have no further use for me. It was all over. Our love had been an illusion.

Swaths of mist rolled in from the sea. The water's loud, tormented sound matched my own tortured spirit and drew me to it. Hot tears followed down my cheeks and were whipped away by the quickening wind. A warning flash of lightning lit the sky and answering thunder drowned out my sobs. The storm was a perfect accompaniment to my own misery. I stumbled down the steep path to the beach.

Sunk in heartache and despair, I wanted to lose myself in the warring elements. I did not want to think or remember as I trudged along in the deep sand along the narrow stretch of beach. A few warning drops of rain touched my hot face and sprays of arching water warned me that my path was growing smaller and smaller. Suddenly I stopped.

It was not sound nor movement but an inner sense that made me jerk suddenly around. I brushed aside the strands of hair clinging to my face. In the distance the familiar black horse which Adam always rode raced along the water's edge toward me. The rider was whipping the mount so that it rushed at me with deadly speed.

He's going to run me down!

"No, Adam, no!" My usefulness as a hostage bride was over. I was no longer needed. He had what he wanted.

There was no place for me to flee. The high cliffs on one side and the pounding surf on the other had me trapped on a narrow strip of sand. Instinctively I began running even though I knew it was hopeless. I could not outrun Midnight. The stallion's trampling hooves were closing the distance between us.

I cried out. A spear of jagged lightning cut across the shrouded sky. The storm had given its warning and I had not heeded it. I had been lost in my own thoughts and now it was too late to turn back. A sheet of gray rain blinded me as I lunged forward, my long skirts whipping around my legs and encumbering my flight.

There was no escape. I could not scale the sheer cliffs which offered no footing! But if I did not leave the narrow ledge of sand, I would be trampled to death. Only the treacherous white-capped water, pounding against jagged rocks glistening in the rolling sea, offered a momentary sanctuary.

I plunged into the cold waters and instantly was swept off my feet by the pounding surf. Whipped by a vicious undertow, I kicked my arms and legs, struggling to retain some control as the water swept me away from the shore. Like a rudderless boat tossed up and down in the rolling water, I could not keep myself from being swept into a churning maelstrom. My weighted gown and petticoat hampered my thrusting legs. It would be impossible to keep afloat for more than a few seconds.

A huge wave lifted me up and filled my eyes and nose with water so that I could not see nor breathe. As the current swept me into a circle of rocks, I clutched at one of them. My fingers fastened on a jagged edge. With a strength born out of terror, I held on. Momentarily, my grip on it kept me from being pounded against the rocky outcropping. If I let loose, I would be swept out to sea, a drowning victim. There would be no evidence of foul play if my body was ever recovered.

Till death do us part! The remembered phrase pounded relentlessly in my ears . . . a mockery to a love I could not deny even now. Suddenly the struggle for life did not seem worth the effort. "Adam . . . Adam!" I sobbed and let my tired hands slip away from the rock.

At first, I thought that the firm thrust of my body through the water was caused by the tongues of an undertown. Then I realized that the vise-like grip around my waist was human and that the arms that lifted me out of the water were familiar. I opened my eyes. Through rivulets of water and drenched tendrils of hair, I saw Adam's face close to mine. His loving expression was not the face of a murderer . . . but of a man who would risk everything to save his beloved.

"Darling . . . darling!" he murmured as he laid me gently on the warm sand.

I looked up at the man mounted on Midnight, the halter firmly held by Jasper.

Larry!

His round face was like leather and his expression ugly. He glared at me as if hate would snuff the breath from my heaving chest. "Why?" I croaked.

"Later," said my beloved husband. And he picked me up in his arms and set me on the sorrel mare which had brought him to my rescue.

* * *

That night, propped up in bed with soft pillows, I ate my dinner from a tray as Adam hovered over me and promised that he would answer all my questions when the last bite was taken.

"What happened today was the very thing I have been trying to avoid," he said when I was finished. "I didn't want to put you in any danger. Your ignorance was your protection. How could I have known that the professor was going to put the new blueprint in your hands? If only you had told me—"

"How could I when I knew you were here to steal them?"

"But not for any avaricious reason. I was sent here to get them back. You see the plans are really the property of the United States government. Professor Lynwood was paid for his invention. He was working for our defense department but when his long-awaited experiment failed, he became angry at the ridicule he received and decided he would not turn over the corrected plans to our government. We couldn't let them reach foreign hands. I was given the assignment of getting them back. With the blessing of the President, I might add."

"Then my father was never in any danger? You lied to me!"

"Yes," he said with infuriating frankness. "You're a terrible actress, darling. You would have betrayed yourself to the professor if you had known the true situation. Only by getting close to the Professor could we make certain a foreign power didn't get possession of the scientist's valuable invention."

"But Larry—?"

"We had evidence that Larry was making contact with some foreign governments concerning the sale of his uncle's invention. He played on his uncle's anger, persuading him to take the plans out of the country. But in the end, the Professor couldn't do it and he fouled up Larry's chance to sell them. He decided to send them back to the United States with you. Without telling Larry, he hid the drawing in the photograph album and gave it to you to take back to your father. I didn't expect anything like that to happen. I just knew that you were the one who could get me close to the professor."

"What if he had taken a dislike to me?"

He grinned. "We made certain that you were perfect for the job. Too perfect as it turned out. I never expected him to hand the document over to you the way he did. I thought I could keep you out of it. As long as you thought I was a jewel thief, there was no danger of getting you involved in my true mission."

"I should have known that you couldn't have arranged everything so smoothly all by yourself."

He nodded. "A lot of people worked out the details. We learned that your father had been good friends with Professor Lynwood and that you would be traveling on the same ship with him. Your Cousin Della was arrested so she would be out of the way. She and her husband had been engaged in illicit smuggling for years. She might have involved you in that latest caper with the Havershams. We know that she had been paid to smuggle the emeralds out of the country for them."

"That's why they accepted them from me."

"Right."

"Only you turned them in."

"Right again."

"You knew all about Cousin Della . . . and me . . . and my father—"

"That's my business. I'm not a lawyer. I work for the United States National Security. And I was chosen to carry out the hostage plan, marry you, and make certain that we were invited here on our honeymoon. It was to be a platonic arrangement—" He touched a light kiss to my forehead. "—but I fell in love. Which only made my job harder. We knew that Larry had already made overtures to the German government to sell his uncle's invention to them. And it turned out that Freddy Heinlin was here at Lynwood Manor to negotiate the deal.

"Freddy!"

Adam nodded. "That day in London at Hyde Park, I met with a man from Scotland Yard. He confirmed what I had suspected on the Lucania. Freddy Heinlin had struck up a friendship with Pamela as a cover. Unfortunately, Pamela thought he was really attracted to her, but it was just a ruse dreamed up by Larry and Freddy so he could be here at Lynwood Hall when the Professor decided to turn the plans over to the Germans."

"But Professor Lynwood changed his mind, didn't he? He decided to send the plans back to the United States with me. He probably would have written a letter to my father and told him where he'd hidden the picture."

"Yes. He must have told Larry that he'd changed his mind and then, on the night of the party, unexpectedly came upon his nephew in his study looking for the document."

"But how did Larry know the drawing was in the album?"

"His uncle was still rambling about the album and your mother's picture when he visited him just after you saw the Professor this morning."

My eyes widened. "He was visiting his uncle at the time I was going out to the garden."

Adam nodded. "He must have seen you with the album. When his uncle rambled on about it, he quickly found you in the garden, hit you on the head, and then came back to the stables and saddled up Midnight."

"But I saw Jasper talking with you and I thought he had been watching me with the album."

"He was. He saw what happened. Told me that Larry had taken something from you. That was the first time I realized that the document I was looking for had been hidden in the album. You little fool! If you had just turned the document over to me! Instead you nearly got yourself drowned. When Larry saw you so vulnerable, he couldn't resist making certain you didn't cause any more trouble."

Fortunately Adam had seen Larry racing on the beach and followed him. "I got there just as you were slipping away from that rock." He threaded my hair through his fingers and lifted my chin. He kissed me with a fierce passion that betrayed the fright he had suffered when he saw me struggling in the water.

There were no more shadows between us but I could not resist one last accusation. When he stopped kissing me long enough to let me catch my breath, I murmured, "I still don't know why you weren't honest with me. You let me think you were after my aunt's emeralds, Pamela's jewels, and that you were an unscrupulous traitor after the professor's invention."

"Yes." His mouth curved in that devastating smile, his mouth hovering above mine.

"I think you're perfectly detestable . . . horrid . . . and loathsome!"

"Really?" He circled me with his arms. "Charl, you're a terrible liar."

The heat of his body spiraled into mine. His eyes were a soft, caressing blue and I was drawn into their warm depths. "Show me again, Mrs. Demorest . . . just how much you hate me."

And I did.

TIMESWEPT ROMANCE

TIME OF THE ROSE
By Bonita Clifton

When the silver-haired cowboy brings Madison Calloway to his run-down ranch, she thinks for sure he is senile. Certain he'll bring harm to himself, Madison follows the man into a thunderstorm and back to the wild days of his youth in the Old West.

The dread of all his enemies and the desire of all the ladies, Colton Chase does not stand a chance against the spunky beauty who has tracked him through time. And after one passion-drenched night, Colt is ready to surrender his heart to the most tempting spitfire anywhere in time.

_51922-4 $4.99 US/$5.99 CAN

A FUTURISTIC ROMANCE

AWAKENINGS
By Saranne Dawson

Fearless and bold, Justan rules his domain with an iron hand, but nothing short of the Dammai's magic will bring his warring people peace. He claims he needs Rozlynd—a bewitching beauty and the last of the Dammai—for her sorcery alone, yet inside him stirs an unexpected yearning to savor the temptress's charms, to sample her sweet innocence. And as her silken spell ensnares him, Justan battles to vanquish a power whose like he has never encountered—the power of Rozlynd's love.

_51921-6 $4.99 US/$5.99 CAN

LOVE SPELL
ATTN: Order Department
Dorchester Publishing Co., Inc.
276 5th Avenue, New York, NY 10001

Please add $1.50 for shipping and handling for the first book and $.35 for each book thereafter. PA., N.Y.S. and N.Y.C. residents, please add appropriate sales tax. No cash, stamps, or C.O.D.s. All orders shipped within 6 weeks via postal service book rate. Canadian orders require $2.00 extra postage and must be paid in U.S. dollars through a U.S. banking facility.

Name_____
Address_____
City _____ State _____ Zip_____
I have enclosed $_____in payment for the checked book(s).
Payment **must** accompany all orders.☐ Please send a free catalog.